Hugh Coleman Davidson

The Old Adam

A tale of an army crammer. Vol. 2

Hugh Coleman Davidson

The Old Adam
A tale of an army crammer. Vol. 2

ISBN/EAN: 9783337344481

Printed in Europe, USA, Canada, Australia, Japan

Cover: Foto ©Andreas Hilbeck / pixelio.de

More available books at **www.hansebooks.com**

THE OLD ADAM.

A TALE OF AN ARMY CRAMMER.

BY

HUGH COLEMAN DAVIDSON,

AUTHOR OF

"THE GREEN HILLS BY THE SEA," "CAST ON THE WATERS," ETC.

IN THREE VOLUMES.
VOL. II.

LONDON:
SAMPSON LOW, MARSTON, SEARLE, & RIVINGTON,
LIMITED,
St. Dunstan's House,
FETTER LANE, FLEET STREET, E.C.
1888.

LONDON :

PRINTED BY WILLIAM CLOWES AND SONS, LIMITED,
STAMFORD STREET AND CHARING CROSS.

CONTENTS OF VOL. II.

———•◦•———

THE OLD ADAM.

CHAPTER I.

TOO LATE.

BEFORE Philip could reach the gate, the French beggar had joined Mr. Valentine Gaunt, who appeared to have been waiting for him in the garden. This oddly-matched couple must have nearly finished their conversation, for scarcely a word passed between them. Surprised at the man's disappearance through the gateway, Philip had stopped to look over the wall; and saw that some money was given by the one to the other. But the next moment two pairs of eyes were fastened upon him, and, feeling that he was playing

VOL. II.   B

the spy, he withdrew; only to return with the intention of frankly showing himself.

When he looked again, Mr. Valentine Gaunt, with his hands in his pockets, was smoking his big meerschaum on the lawn, while his seedy acquaintance had vanished.

A smartly-dressed page appeared at the door and made obeisance.

"Lunch is ready, sir," he announced. The Hive was not remarkable for punctuality.

"Very well, John," said Mr. Valentine Gaunt, regarding the youth with the pride of recent proprietorship; though it must be added that John led a frightful life among so many masters. "Tell Mrs. Smith"—the housekeeper—"that I am going to London this afternoon and shall not return until to-morrow. She is to pack my bag for one night. And now ring the bell."

"Yes, sir," said John, and departed on his mission.

When Mr. Valentine Gaunt had knocked the ashes out of his pipe, he sauntered in to lunch, which had already commenced without

him. It was part of his method, but it sometimes resulted in his faring rather badly, and
it never failed to ruffle his temper. In fact,
he found it difficult to drop the master in
some things and retain it in others, the pupils
were so lamentably wanting in discrimination.
In consequence, meals at the Hive were
terrible scrambles, costing the Professor many
a groan as he saw his favourite delicacies
appropriated by these selfish young fellows
before he could get a chance.

To-day, thanks to the coach, there was no
great crush, and yet it was noticed that he
was not in the best of tempers. Though it
was his habit to assume at times an air of
philosophic abstraction which threw his
lighter moods into strong relief, he was
unusually silent at table, and it was very
soon whispered about that "something was
up." This became all the clearer when he
announced his intention of going to London.

Lectures were over for the day, Wednesday
being a half-holiday, but he arranged for the
work of the following morning. Then he

wrote a note, explaining to the Doctor that he was called away by urgent business ; and, after a quiet smoke, took his bag in his hand and strolled up to the Lark's-Nest to get a trap.

"Dog-cart at once for Stilbury," he said, entering the yard.

The man thus addressed turned round with a start, for he had not heard any one coming; so softly had that stealthy footstep fallen upon the stone pavement. He was a little thick-set man, with stubbly red hair, a very freckled complexion, and a turned-up nose— a stranger to Mr. Valentine Gaunt—in fact, he had been engaged by Mr. Smirke only that morning. His shirt-sleeves were rolled up to his elbows, and he was carrying a bucket and a mop, which he now set down.

"Dog-cart for Stilbury, sir. Yes, sir," said he, touching his cap. He began to bustle about the yard, but soon returned to add, "If you please, sir, I was to ask you for your order."

"My order!" exclaimed Mr. Valentine

Gaunt, for he had not yet heard of the Doctor's arrangements. "Great heavens, man! what do you mean?"

"I'm not very clear myself, sir. Master said an order signed by the Doctor or Mr. Sterne, I think the name was, and I wasn't to let no one go without it."

The matter was plain enough now. Mr. Valentine Gaunt felt that a gross indignity had been put upon him by the Doctor. Here he was publicly proclaimed to be on a lower level than Sterne. His cheek-bones were ablaze with rage.

"You blundering idiot!" he cried. "I'm not a pupil, I'm a tutor—Mr. Valentine Gaunt."

"Can't help that, sir," replied the man doggedly. "Them's my orders."

"Confound your insolence! You shall be discharged for this, my man. Where is Mr. Smirke?"

"He's at Stilbury, sir."

"Where is Albert, then?"

"Driving the fly, sir."

" Goodness gracious ! Who is in charge of the yard ? "

" I am, sir."

Here was a pleasant predicament for a learned Professor. The man answered civilly enough, but as he stood there twisting his cap round his fingers, with the sunlight falling upon his red hair and freckled face, he looked the very embodiment of stubbornness. Mr. Valentine Gaunt ripped his watch out of his pocket, and saw that in another twenty minutes he would have no chance of catching the train.

" I can't afford to waste my time here," he said desperately. " Once more I tell you that my name is Valentine Gaunt ; that I am a tutor, and not a pupil ; and that the rule you mention doesn't apply to me. Now, do you understand ? Come, my good fellow, bustle about and get that dog-cart sharp."

" You've heard my orders, sir," returned the man, still twisting his cap round his fingers ; " you must go to them as gave them."

" You obstinate fool ! "

" You call yourself a gentleman. I suppose, sir ? " said the man, without the least intention of irony. " Well, I wasn't to let no gentleman go. Them's my orders, sir."

Perhaps Mr. Valentine Gaunt might have escaped through this loophole without laying any great burden on his conscience, but in a towering rage he flung his bag into a corner of the yard, and strode off towards the Rectory.

Gammon, in a blue apron, and with a cleaver in his hand, stood in the doorway and touched his hat as that tall, strong, round-shouldered figure went by ; Whittle looked after him curiously, wondering whether any accident had befallen the big meerschaum, without which he was seldom seen. Joseph Haply heaved at him a word of greeting, and from among the greenery already spread around the lattice windows, faces smiled pleasantly at the man who had become a power in their midst. They honestly liked him, for he never showed his teeth except to those who stood in his way. This, again, was part of his method.

But, affable as he could be when he chose, he paid no heed to anybody now; merely strode on with a determined purpose. In front of the Hut he came face to face with Leonard Sterne. He stopped at once.

"Ha!" he said, scowling from beneath his heavy brows. "What's the meaning of this—this impertinent rule about orders, Mr. Sterne?"

"The Doctor is responsible for all the rules here, Mr. Gaunt. I don't know which you allude to."

"That blockhead in Smirke's yard has refused me a trap because I am unprovided with an order from the Doctor, or Mr. Sterne, forsooth. Before I can leave Puddleton, I must ask permission of the Rev. Leonard Sterne. I am told this by a low stableman. Is it a practical joke for the benefit of the village?"

"The Doctor didn't consult me in the matter," said Sterne quietly. "I must refer you to him, Mr. Gaunt."

" Indeed," said the other, in his most insolent manner. He was almost beside himself with rage.

Sterne's long face relaxed into a smile. He could no longer resist the temptation of giving this irritating man a playful dig in the ribs, imprudent as it was.

" Meanwhile," he said blandly, " until you have set matters right with the Doctor, will you allow me to give you an order?"

For a moment this speech seemed to have taken Mr. Valentine Gaunt's breath away. He could do nothing but stare. Then his eyes blazed up with diabolical hatred, and he hissed out—

" Some day you will be sorry for this, you wolf in sheep's clothing."

It would have been some consolation if he had goaded the clergyman into losing his temper, but Sterne merely turned on his heel and continued his way towards the Lark's-Nest. He also was going to London, and would gladly have offered the other a seat in his trap, but anything of the sort was now impossible. He felt sorry that he had yielded to the impulse to say something sharp; it was not the first time that he had unintentionally widened the breach, but his nature contained a certain amount of acidity which he had not altogether got rid of when he put on the cassock, and it was the more difficult to control in private on account of the strong restraint that he laid upon his tongue in public.

Mr. Valentine Gaunt stood looking after Sterne, and then went on to the Rectory, where he spent an hour in badgering the Doctor. He resembled a large clock running down after the pendulum had been removed. He struck but one note, and that note was Leonard Sterne. It was not a new character for him to appear in; he had already shown himself to be a bully, but not of such a pronounced type as now; he had advanced another step, and that was all.

The Doctor's face was a pitiable sight. It had aged sadly, as it seemed in some strange way to do when his will was overpowered.

His thin fingers were nervously passing
through and through his grey hair, and as
he hung over his writing-table, he looked a
tired-out old man; but when the abuse of his
friend ended in a demand for his dismissal,
he gathered himself together with the resolu-
tion of despair. No doubt he was partly
influenced by motives of self-interest, knowing
that the establishment in which all his ambition was centred would infallibly fall to the
ground if he were to lose Leonard Sterne,
who possessed in a very high degree the
powers of management, in which Mr. Valentine Gaunt was utterly deficient; but mingled
with this feeling was a determination to
stand by the trusty lieutenant who had stood
by him.

Mr. Valentine Gaunt, who had been watching the Doctor with steady eyes and hovering
foot, was quick to notice the change and shift
his ground. He glided away to another topic,
and did not again recur to the old one. In
fact, he still showed remarkable indecision in
pressing a point home. When he eventually

left the Rectory, he looked anything but satisfied with himself. Conscious of having shown weakness, he feared that the Doctor might some day avail himself of it and summon up enough courage to advance. Essentially a coward, Mr. Valentine Gaunt was very apt to take alarm at the least sign of resistance, and, indeed, at the opportunity for it.

In the village he met Hebe Pike, who blushed and smiled at him with a very pretty shyness. His manner towards her was one of kindly patronage, yet he watched her much as a doctor watches a patient in a critical condition. Her brown eyes fell before his earnest gaze, and she prattled away at a great rate in order to cover her confusion. When he told her where he was going, this brisk young lady whisked a letter from her pocket.

" I kept it ready," she said, " and now I'll fasten it." Which she accordingly did, and then handed it to him.

"Now that Arnold is getting on," said

Mr. Valentine Gaunt, complacently stroking his whiskers, " don't you think—eh ? "

"Really, Mr. Gaunt," said Hebe, not at all displeased at his mysterious suggestion, though she turned her back upon him.

"But it's about time to do something."

"Really, Mr. Gaunt."

"Well, think it over, Miss Hebe. If a friend can help you, you know where to find him. Good afternoon. You shall have your answer to-morrow."

He found a dog-cart waiting for him in Smirke's yard, Higgins having been despatched by the Doctor to explain matters to the obstinate ostler, who was now very profuse in his apologies; and in less than an hour he was at Stilbury, where he was received with the same ceremony as on a previous occasion. As he had driven over alone, the dog-cart was sent to the Cygnet, an old-fashioned inn near the station, with instructions that it should be ready for him when he returned on the following afternoon.

It was nearly six o'clock before Mr. Valentine Gaunt arrived in London. After making perfectly certain that there was no one else from Puddleton in the train, he engaged a hansom and drove straight to Momus Street, but at the corner he cautiously alighted. He had displayed much uneasiness during the journey, and an altercation with the driver about the fare did not improve his temper. However, not caring to attract notice, he paid what the man demanded, and walked slowly on to his destination.

Suddenly he stopped and changed colour— there were bills in the windows of No. 13. The house was deserted ; it looked like a blind man from whose eyes the light has died out for ever. The dust lay thickly on the panes, and two of them were broken already. No matter how great the desolation, if only there be unprotected glass, there is sure to be some British urchin ready with a stone.

For Mr. Valentine Gaunt this forsaken house had a horribly mocking aspect. He detected malice in the blankly-staring windows; he heard it in the breeze rustling the straw and papers in the area; the very figures which some ingenious young artist had traced in the dust upon the door, seemed to be grinning at him ; even the chirping of an impudent sparrow in the roadway added to his irritation. He was so angry that he clenched his fist and shook it at the house.

A street Arab came whistling by—a bright, merry little fellow, in spite of his tattered clothes which scarcely held together. Mr. Valentine Gaunt asked him whether he knew how long the tenants had gone. He replied that he did not, but there was an auctioneer's at the corner. Would the kind gentleman give him a copper ? No, the kind gentleman would do nothing of the sort. Though there had been a hungry longing in his brown face, the little fellow laughed and whistled on merrily again, leaving Mr. Valentine Gaunt moodily studying the bills in the windows.

When at length he turned away, he discovered that he was being watched by a

figure standing on the opposite side of the
street—a slim athletic figure, with a long
brown beard, an austere type of face, a black
coat, and a hat with a broad brim and a
tassel.

His first impulse was to dash across the
street and give free vent to his feelings, but
he checked himself, pausing until he felt able
to keep to his method. Then he advanced so
slowly that each foot hung a very perceptible
time in the air.

" So you have followed me here, Mr.
Sterne," he sneered.

" I feared you might think so, Mr. Gaunt,"
said Sterne very quietly, " when I un-
expectedly saw you on the other side of the
street, and for that reason I waited, to explain
if you wished. I preceded you to London."

" And waited at the station."

" I need scarcely deny that. You are the
last person I should have expected to find
here."

" Ditto, Mr. Sterne."

" Your tone," said Sterne, looking fearlessly

at the sinister face that was watching him with such an insolent expression, "is not one to encourage a friendly explanation, but here it is, nevertheless. I have been visiting a good old soul, to whom I am indebted for much motherly care—for my life, in fact. She was nurse in my father's family, and now lives in Bloomsbury, where I go to see her occasionally. There is nothing very strange in that."

"Oh dear, no," rasped out Mr. Valentine Gaunt. "Nothing strange at all. So you have been visiting a good old soul, have you, Mr. Sterne? And being a charitable giver, you have been sneaking through the most deserted streets, I suppose."

"Do you claim the monopoly of all the deserted streets?" inquired Sterne, with a smile. "I have told you it was an accident."

"I don't believe a word of your lies," roared the Professor of English. "Not one word of them. You profess to like candour, Mr. Sterne. Here it is; here is my candid opinion of you. You're a sneaking, hypo-

critical spy, nothing more nor less; a con-
founded sneaking, canting, hypocritical spy,
sir."

"Then I shall not trouble you when I
want a testimonial," laughed Sterne, stepping
back to put temptation out of the way of the
other's restless hand.

"Oh, I wouldn't hurt you," said Mr.
Valentine Gaunt, after a swift glance of apprehension, for the shaft had stung him more
than he cared to show. "I wouldn't touch a
hair of your head. Gentlemen, Mr. Sterne
—gentlemen fight only with gentlemen."

"I didn't know they fought at all, Mr.
Gaunt. But now that you have enlightened
me, I am glad to hear that there is some bar
to promiscuous brawling."

Mr. Valentine Gaunt retreated a few paces
in order to get a better look at the clergyman. It was his method of showing unutter-
able contempt. When he had finished his
survey, he did what he felt sorry for in his
cooler moments—walked to one side and
pointed to the house opposite.

"Too late," he sneered; "too late, you clerical hypocrite. Your pretended ignorance won't deceive me. What I first thought a calamity has turned out to be a blessing. I'll wish you good afternoon, Mr. Sterne."

When left alone, Leonard Sterne remained for some time in the same attitude, thinking deeply. He was engaged in a keen debate with himself as to how he should act. Puzzled as he was, he felt that chance had brought him to the threshold of a mystery, which he was anxious to explore, but he doubted whether he ought to proceed considering all the circumstances. He was still haunted by the dread of doing anything out of jealous rivalry or personal feeling; he had so long been the Doctor's lieutenant as to regard himself as a piece of the machinery at Puddleton rather than as an individual with independent sensations; and so he had grown into the habit of considering how each action of his would influence the whole. In the present case, when he reflected how widely spread was the disorder among the pupils,

and what a terror Mr. Valentine Gaunt had
become to the Doctor, his scruples vanished.
He resolved to utilize what he conceived to
be his opportunity.   First of all, he would
make an attempt to trace the late tenants of
the house opposite, and after that, pay a visit
to the maker of the court wig in Parnassus
Street.   In fact, he would henceforth do his
utmost to rid the Doctor of Mr. Valentine
Gaunt.

Sterne began by crossing the street to read
the bills in the windows.   They referred
inquirers to the auctioneer's at the corner.
So thither he went next.

CHAPTER II.

AFTER repeated failures, Arnold's efforts were eventually successful. He was engaged for a very minor part in a very minor theatre. As he afterwards came to be rather ashamed of the place where he made his *début*, perhaps the less said about it the better; but it was at any rate a beginning, which drove M. Dubarri almost frantic with delight. His feelings, however, were not entirely disinterested, for he knew that his mysterious pupil, who received no letters, and seemed to have neither friend nor relative, must be getting towards the end of his resources.

On the night of the first performance, M. Dubarri—dressed in very baggy trousers, and a blue frock-coat, showing an immense amount of shirt-front, with his gold-rimmed *pince-nez* dangling outside, and a flower, in addition to the ribbon of the Legion of Honour, in his button-hole—occupied a seat in the front row of the stalls and applauded his pupil most vociferously. His enthusiasm was so catching that many others began to follow his example, and it was singular that his applause always found an immediate echo in one corner of the gallery.

But M. Dubarri did not stop here. During the intervals he spoke loudly to those around him about the marked ability shown by that rising young actor, Mr. Arnold Cressingham. It was a great pity, he said, that he should have been cast for so small a part, but no doubt his merits would be speedily recognized by the managers of West End houses. Lest it should be supposed that he was acting in collusion with the man he was praising, he sent his card round to Arnold, with the hope that he might have the honour of an interview after the performance.

The meeting at the stage-door was affectionate enough to impress the beholders. Indeed, they were rather inclined to laugh, when M. Dubarri rushed forward and clasped Arnold to his breast. The latter did not like the situation at all. He struggled to get free, but, big fellow as he was, could not release himself from the grasp of the active little Frenchman, who was all the time calling two languages to testify to the ability of this phenomenal young actor. On the road home he insisted upon embracing Arnold at frequent intervals, and often stopped to shake hands.

There was a quiet little publichouse next door to the auctioneer's at the corner of Momus Street, and here M. Dubarri purchased an eighteen-penny bottle of claret, which he carried home with as much tender pride as if it had been his own baby. He was disappointed that Arnold did not show the same childlike enthusiasm on the subject, but he soon got over that, for he was pretty well accustomed to Arnold's manner by this time.

They found supper awaiting them. It consisted of a Bologna sausage, part of an American cheese, a plate of onions, and some butter and bread. From his lordly way of placing the bottle of claret on the table, M. Dubarri evidently considered it a sumptuous feast. Before they began, he again embraced Arnold, and after that felt better able to attack the Bologna sausage.

—"Now," said M. Dubarri, carefully laying his knife and fork in the same straight line, with their extremities resting upon the opposite edge of his plate, "pass your glass, my friend."

He always filled Arnold's glass himself, not from stinginess, for he was a very generous old fellow when he had any money, which was not often, but from fear lest the precious bottle should be shaken. While he was pouring out the wine, his forehead was wrinkled up like the sand on the sea-shore, and even his funny little snub nose seemed to join with his other features in an expression of intense concentration. When his task was completed, he heaved a deep sigh, smiled as he took up his glass, and then his keen small eyes blinked pleasantly through it.

"I drink to you, my friend," said M. Dubarri, holding his glass aloft. He took a few sips and smacked his lips. "Ah, ha!" he cried. "It is good—eh?"

"Excellent."

"I think so. I am a judge, you know. Yes, I flatter myself I know a little about wine, and this is very good. It has no need of the bush, as your English proverb says. I drink to you again, my friend. Success!"

"And money," drawled Arnold, twirling his moustache.

"That is sure, for they go together. Ah! you will be rich; never fear. Your acting was superb, magnificent. *Sapristi!* it electrified the house. The applause was immense, I do assure you."

"I noticed that it came chiefly from the front row of the stalls," said Arnold, slowly lifting his grey eyes to M. Dubarri's, and reflecting the smile that he saw therein.

It was, however, rather a dubious smile in M. Dubarri's case. He was blinking in a puzzled way at the phlegmatic young man whom he had not yet learnt to understand—whom he never would understand if they were to live together for a century.

"Your friends will be pleased at your success," he said, watching keenly.

"No doubt."

"You will write to tell them?"

"Why should I, when they can read about it in the newspapers?"

"You are a strange fellow, Mr. Arnold. It is difficult to get to the bottom of you. I am frank, you see, as usual. Eh bien! you are clever, I think, and will succeed. My friend, I shake you by the hand." Whereupon M. Dubarri precipitated himself across the room.

They had many of these pleasant little suppers, for the Professor seemed to think that he could never do enough for his successful pupil, whose very reticence about himself was an attraction. He was continually bringing in some delicacy under his arm, or else in his coat-pocket. Sometimes, as a rare treat, it was a tin of *pâté de foie gras*, sometimes a pound of ham, sometimes a pint of shrimps; but the parcel was always produced with the same air of important mystery and opened with the same exuberant delight. Arnold being disappointingly undemonstrative, M. Dubarri never failed to pronounce each article to be good, and himself to be a judge of it.

These were not unhappy days; indeed, it was hard to be unhappy in M. Dubarri's company, though he had little enough to laugh about, goodness knows. He was one of those who can make a respectable show on almost nothing, a secret possessed by none but Frenchmen, and only by a few of them; but as he was very reserved about money matters, it may safely be said that they were at a terribly low ebb. Of course, he got a few pounds from Arnold; then he had an occasional pupil or so; and he did a little quiet trading in cheap jewelry on his own account.

But he never would talk about his means·—
always turned the subject; and if any of his
compatriots, paying him a friendly visit,
happened to be in a desponding mood, threw
himself body and soul into the task of cheering them up.

The only time when he ever displayed the
least uneasiness, was in the presence of Mr.
Valentine Gaunt, who seemed to be playing
simultaneously upon two very similar instru-
ments, the one in London and the other in
Puddleton.   He had a masterful way of
marching into No. 13, Momus Street, just as
he did into the Rectory; from his general
behaviour he might have been taken for the
owner of both houses.   Neither of the rightful
owners had the courage to object to what
irritated them exceedingly; both met his
advances by retreating before him; and so
he proceeded, step by step, to a position of
authority, which was very perplexing to
outsiders.

He and Arnold had been formally introduced by M. Dubarri, who was unaware of

their previous acquaintance, and they had since been on very friendly terms. Several letters had been handed by the one to the other, but always in the passage when no one was about. In this way Arnold had contrived to keep up a correspondence with Hebe, who had pardoned his long silence, because—well, simply because she was in love with him.

It is unnecessary to emphasize his faults, they are so conspicuous, but most of them had a common origin in indolent selfishness. It had led him to disregard the feelings of his father and sister, partly, it must be said, because he compared them with his own, and so underestimated their depth; it had led him to think that Hebe would patiently endure his silence while he was working to bring about their marriage, not by gentle persuasion, but in direct opposition to the Doctor's wish; and it was leading him now to deceive M. Dubarri by his pretended ignorance of Mr. Valentine Gaunt. However, trouble is a tolerably effective cure for selfishness, and few of us escape that in time.

Mr. Valentine Gaunt was very pleased when he heard of Arnold's success ; he made a high-flown speech in which he congratulated the young actor warmly. There was an odd smile on his face : a smile that attracted no particular notice from Arnold, but puzzled M. Dubarri, who took the speech as a compliment to himself and listened, blinking delightedly. It seemed to hide something—to be continually under restraint lest it should break into unmethodical significance ; and this it did as soon as Mr. Valentine Gaunt found himself alone in the street. But several months later, at the close of the pantomime season, he was not quite so hearty in his congratulations upon learning that Arnold had been promoted to the position of a "walking gentleman"—or, rather, a footman —on the boards of the Parnassus. It struck him that the young actor—who, notwithstanding his impassiveness, showed considerable ability in reflecting the feelings, just as

he did the smiles, of others—was getting on
a little too rapidly; he was not certain how
matters would look from the front. So, after
pointing out that his method of "slow and
sure" was the best in the long run, he went
back to Puddleton to think it over.

Of course, M. Dubarri was in the wildest
glee. He again sat in the front row of the
stalls and applauded the footman vehemently;
again embraced him at the stage-door; and
again led him rapturously home to an inviting
little supper, part of which was the inevitable
bottle of claret. There is not the smallest
doubt that he considered it his own triumph
quite as much as his pupil's; in fact, when
Arnold failed to propose M. Dubarri's health,
M. Dubarri, after waiting with an expectant
air, which at length yielded to a look of
gentle reproach, modestly got up and proposed
his own.

For the next few weeks he was in high
feather; and then the uneasiness which had
been alluded to, seemed to grow upon him.
He became extremely fidgety, trotting about

the room without any definite purpose and all the while casting furtive glances at Arnold, as if he was trying to make up his mind to some decisive step. It was one afternoon, while he was sitting in the arm-chair and Arnold on the couch opposite, the two being in an unusually confidential mood, that he announced his intention.

"What do you think of Mr. Valentine Gaunt?" he asked cautiously.

"Well, really, M. Dubarri, you have done all my thinking so long that I have quite got out of the way of it."

"Vous plaisantez toujours," exclaimed M. Dubarri, with a gesture of impatience. "Come, my friend, I shall give you my opinion, for you know I am frank. You smile, you big fellow, you. Eh bien! no matter. I am not a bad judge of character, and I tell you this: Mr. Valentine Gaunt is a good fellow in his way, but between ourselves he is rather a rascal."

Arnold looked up, but his eyes fell immediately, and he said nothing.

" That is right, I do assure you," continued
M. Dubarri. " He is a heavy ruffian, without
doubt. If I were to look for an English
phrase for him, I should call him a beetle-
crusher. Scrunch — so." He stamped
viciously at the carpet with his heel. " I
think there would not be much left of that
fellow if he had been underneath," added he,
alluding, probably, to some imaginary beetle.
" Let me advise you one thing, my friend.
If you have a secret, keep it. Never tell it
to Mr. Valentine Gaunt—never—never—or
you may be sorry."

Arnold remembered that Mr. Valentine
Gaunt had used almost the same words of
M. Dubarri.

" I have told him something," proceeded
M. Dubarri, coming a little more forward in
his chair, " and I am sorry. He does not
know all, it is true, but he wants to know
more and bothers me. He is a dreadful
fellow, that beetle-crushing Mr. Valentine
Gaunt who creeps upon one like a cat.
Sapristi ! I would escape from him—go away

on the sly—leave no tracks, no scent, no footprints, nothing. I would run away, you understand, not from fear, of course, but just to play him a little trick. Ah! That will be fun, I think. While he is sniffing around Momus Street, we shall be laughing in our beards. How he will rage, to be sure!" At the thought of such an excellent joke, M. Dubarri went off into a peal of laughter—a perfect convulsion it was, shaking him internally even when no sound was coming from his lips.

"But," said Arnold, "surely it is a great deal of trouble for a very little fun."

"Do you object?"

"Not at all, if you wish it."

"You are a good fellow, and I shake you by the hand," said M. Dubarri, suiting the action to the word. "Then it is settled; we shall go to-morrow. I take this house furnished by the month, you know, and the month will be finished to-morrow. I have been to look at another house in the Harrow Road, Paddington. You will like it, I am

sure. It is snug, that house, far more beautiful than this. Bah! this Momus Street is a
dismal place. It gives me the blues every
hour of the day. You will prefer the Harrow
Road—eh?" he asked, with a look of anxious
interest.

"Oh yes, I am sure to do that," replied
Arnold, with easy good-humour. "So we
leave here to-morrow."

"Sapristi—hush!" cried M. Dubarri, ex-
citedly springing to his feet and clapping his
hand on Arnold's mouth.

Then he ran to the window, which was
slightly open, the weather being warm and
muggy. Arnold looked after him in surprise,
and saw through the aperture a dirty foreign-
looking face with a stubbly grey beard and
half-whining, half-curious expression.

"Qu'y a-t-il, Jacques?" said M. Dubarri
hoarsely.

The reply Arnold did not catch; nor was
he able to follow any of the conversation that
ensued, carried on as it was in whispers.
Indeed, he did not trouble his head about the

matter, but took up a book and began to read. Presently, however, he heard the clink of money, just before the window closed; and then M. Dubarri returned to his seat. He said very little about what had just happened—merely shrugged his shoulders and talked vaguely about a beggar.

" You see, my friend, I am frank," he said, and, with this remark, passed lightly to another subject.

The next day there was a general exodus from No. 13, Momus Street. First of all, a cart carried off the few heavy things belonging to the Histrionic Professor, who had already taken the plate off the door; then the deaf old housekeeper and the pale-faced servant-girl followed in a four-wheeler with more luggage; and lastly, after an animated dispute with the landlord, who claimed compensation for damage to the furniture, but without much success, M. Dubarri and Arnold in another four-wheeler with the rest of the things.

M. Dubarri laughed nearly all the way at the little trick he had played upon Mr.

Valentine Gaunt. And it was only an hour afterwards when the latter and Leonard Sterne actually appeared upon the scene, as already described.

CHAPTER III.

AT SIXES AND SEVENS.

WITHIN a short half-hour two persons called at the auctioneer's, at the corner of Momus Street. The first was Mr. Valentine Gaunt, who wanted to know what had become of the Histrionic Professor, but could not get any information on the subject; the second, the Rev. Leonard Sterne, who learned merely the name of the late tenant of No. 13, for M. Dubarri's frankness had not led him to communicate his future address to anybody in the neighbourhood.

As it was too late to pursue his inquiries any further that night, Sterne walked to the hotel where he was in the habit of staying, dined there, and afterwards visited one of the theatres. It was a mere chance that he did not go to the Parnassus, where he would have seen and probably recognized Arnold, in the guise of a footman. The May meetings were in full swing, and the streets swarmed with ruddy-faced country gentlemen in black coats and white ties : a fact that had perhaps suggested to an enterprising manager that here was an audience to be catered for. At any rate, a very clerical piece was being played at a house close to the Parnassus, and thither Sterne went, sitting in the dress-circle among a goodly array of clergymen, many of whom slept the whole time, the curates quietly, but the rectors snoring loudly.

Next morning, on his way to the station, he called at 26, Parnassus Street, which turned out to be a hairdresser's shop, as he had expected. It contained a large variety of wigs and had a decidedly theatrical appearance.

"I should be much obliged," said Sterne with some hesitation, for he felt altogether out of his element, "if you would kindly tell me whether you ever sold an old-fashioned court wig to a Mr. Valentine Gaunt?"

"Madame Farnienti is away at present," replied a smart young woman with bold black eyes and frizzled hair, "but I'll see what I can do for you, sir." She fetched a bulky volume and laid it upon the counter. "Is he one of our regular customers?" she asked, smiling, as if she would have enjoyed a quiet little flirtation with a clergyman in a tasselled hat.

"That I can't say," he said shortly.

Running her finger down a list of names, she turned over several pages. At length she looked up and said—

"Gaunt, I think, was the name you mentioned. I can't find it here."

"Mr. Valentine Gaunt," said Sterne, preparing to depart. "I am sorry to have given you so much trouble."

"I seem to know the name of Valentine, but I'm sure I never heard the name of Gaunt. If he has been one of our regular customers, perhaps Madame Farnienti might remember him, for I have not been here long."

"Oh, thank you, it doesn't much matter," he said ; and left the shop.

It could scarcely be called a disappointment. Sterne had had no definite object in making these inquiries and consequently had not looked forward to any definite result. The truth of the matter was, he did not know what to do to help his friend, so he was ready to turn over any stone that caught his eye.

He encountered Mr. Valentine Gaunt hovering about at the station. They both travelled in the same train, but in different compartments, Sterne going third-class for the sake of economy, which had now become more imperative than ever, and Mr. Valentine Gaunt first-class, for his own comfort. When they arrived at Stilbury, the dog-cart that the latter had left at the Cygnet was awaiting him at the station, and he was conducted to it by a couple of obsequious porters, one carrying his bag and the other his rug.

Sterne, on the other hand, was allowed to go off to his fly alone. So it was clear that the dwellers in this dismal little town had a very fair notion of how matters were going in Puddleton.

Upon his return, Mr. Valentine Gaunt made a slight change in his tactics. Instead of denouncing Sterne to the Doctor, he said nothing about what had happened in London, and took to " damning him with faint praise." Instead of demanding his dismissal, he set to work to undermine his influence with the pupils, he himself keeping carefully in the background. This method, he felt sure, would sooner or later bring about a catastrophe.

It certainly drove the unfortunate Doctor to distraction. The band that nightly paraded the village was bad enough in a place supposed to be devoted to work; the coach was another nuisance which would have been suppressed had it not been a present from the Countess of Belgravia; the fox-terriers were such an absorbing care to their owners, that books were apt to be neglected; but all these sunk into insignificance beside the fact that Sterne was losing his old power of maintaining discipline. It was a strange thing, which perplexed the Doctor almost as much as it troubled him.

Some very disorderly conduct had taken place among Sterne's classes, and matters were growing desperate, when several of the older and more thoughtful among his pupils came to his assistance. It was a shame, they said, to worry a man who even gave up many of his leisure hours to help them; and, moreover, they were very shortly going up for their examination, and did not intend to have their chances of success spoilt by a few selfish fellows who didn't care whether they passed or not. This argument, which they showed themselves ready to enforce if necessary, was effective in restoring order for a time, but it did not add to Sterne's popularity with the unruly spirits, and, feeling themselves to be under Mr. Valentine Gaunt's protection, they still continued to make occasional sallies.

A curious incident occurred on the day before the candidates went up to London to face the Civil Service Examiners.

Mr. Valentine Gaunt was giving the last nervous polish to his French class in the sitting-room of the Hive—a comfortably-furnished room, with a window at each end and a long table in the centre, round which the pupils were sitting, lounging, standing, and smoking. Any stranger peering through the hazy atmosphere might have taken it for a free-and-easy club, engaged in discussing some congenial topic. Plantagenet, who was not equal to any continuous effort, was drawing caricatures of those around him; while Heavisides, who was present as a mere matter of courtesy, was placidly beaming by his side. Most of the others, however, were really working, Philip Strathclyde among the number. The Professor himself was standing on the hearth-rug, smoking his big meerschaum, and letting drop a precious word at intervals—"the latest tip," in fact.

"I wish particularly," he said, "to direct

your attention to this French passage, for it contains——"

At this moment the Doctor's head popped through the door—

"Ah!" he said, smiling pleasantly all round, "this is what I like. Yes, this is really what I do like. Not a sound; not a murmur. Work—work—work! A capital place for work is Puddleton. Are you satisfied with them, Mr. Gaunt?"

"Quite," croaked the Professor, folding his arms. "My method has been singularly successful."

"Yes, yes, I feel sure of that," interrupted the Doctor, quick to perceive that he was threatened with a speech. "You look in fine condition, Merridale; and you, too, Philip, though I did feel a little anxious about you at one time. It's one comfort to know that we are sending you all fit to the post."

The Professor went on with his French, to which the Doctor—only his head and the Yankee hat showing—stood listening, with a very wise face, a trifle on one side, and with

his little twinkling eyes as full of interest as
if he understood every word. Presently he
saw his chance. Tattlemaine, who was
thoughtfully whittling a stick, was requested
to put it away, and replied that he would in
a moment.

" *Tout-de-suite*," cried the Doctor; and,
having exhausted half of his French vocabu-
lary, was on the point of vanishing when he
caught sight of a sketch that Plantagenet
had just made of him.

It was a spasmodic chuckle from Heavisides
that drew his attention to it. Dashing into
the room, he seized the paper, tore it into
atoms, and flung them into the grate. The
whole thing was done without a word. It
was so sudden as to take everybody completely
by surprise. They did not even know whether
he had acted in anger, for with one of those
sharp transitions that came so naturally to
him he began to chaff Heavisides about getting
thin from overwork.

" I should be very pleased," he said, moving
towards the door, "if all my young friends

who are going up for their examination to-
morrow, would come and have dinner with
me at the Rectory this evening at half-past
seven."

"Thank you, Dr. Copingstone," cried a
chorus of voices.

Before the noise had subsided, he was
flying along the street.

"Well," murmured Heavisides, looking
wonderingly round the table, "he's a queer
old hoss, I'm jiggered if he ain't."

"You don't like being laughed at yourself,
my boy," said Merridale.

"But," put in Silverspoon, "it wasn't a
caricature. It was an excellent portrait."

"Plantagenet," said Mr. Valentine Gaunt,
who had watched this little scene with a
strange smile, "will you draw a portrait of
the Doctor for me?"

"Certainly, Mr. Gaunt," replied Lord
Ernest, flattered by the request.

He had a knack of catching a likeness and
transferring it to paper. It was one of the
things that he could do well without much

trouble, and he consequently delighted in
doing it. In a short time he had drawn an
excellent pen-and-ink sketch of the Doctor,
the Yankee hat and Wellington boots being
recognizable anywhere.

Mr. Valentine Gaunt paid the artist a very
high compliment. Then he carefully folded
up the paper and put it in his pocket. And
after the big meerschaum had been filled and
lighted, the lecture was resumed.

From beginning to end, the affair was
most incomprehensible to Philip, though he
was a sharp lad, and had already guessed
more than was generally suspected. Still, he
knew no reason for connecting the Doctor's
dislike to being photographed with his tearing
up a pen-and-ink sketch. Sterne did so when
told what had happened, but Philip could not
see that either circumstance had anything
to do with Mr. Valentine Gaunt, whom he
regarded without any tangible reason as the
origin of all the troubles in the village.
He was inclined to ascribe the Doctor's act
to eccentricity, resulting from worry, and

this made him all the more anxious about Nellie.

He did not believe that she had changed towards him; he did not believe that she ever would change towards him, and yet he had an uneasy feeling that she had purposely avoided him ever since their meeting in the meadow near the old mill. At any rate, they never had been alone in one another's company since that day—the day of the cabinet council—when Nellie went to the bookcase and took down the family Bible, and it had not been Philip's fault that they had not met, for the young lover had lurked in the most likely places, and simply besieged the Rectory. It was no use, however; Nellie seemed to have altered her hours for going to the different cottages, and when he was waiting for her in one place, she was always in another. It puzzled him a great deal, and frightened him a little, simply because he did not know what he had to encounter; but he soon took heart again, for this bright-eyed lad had one of those happy dispositions that

can almost be said to take a delight in over-
coming difficulties.

Once or twice he caught a glimpse of
Nellie on horseback, with the Doctor. He
saw that when her father flourished his crop,
she bowed her dainty head, and he took off
his hat in return ; but on none of these occasions was he close enough to see her pretty
face, which might have given him some clue.
Then, as the days went on, he determined
to lie in wait for her in the churchyard.
While she was walking by the side of her
Sunday-school class, he could easily find an
opportunity of speaking to her. But here again
he was doomed to disappointment. The
children entered the church without Nellie,
and it was not until the bell was on the point
of stopping that she appeared with her father.
The blue eyes were fixed upon the ground,
but she seemed to feel instinctively that Philip
was standing by one of the moss-grown tomb-
stones near the ancient bell-tower, for she
blushed deeply. Before she passed in, she
looked at him and smiled—a sweet smile, but

oh, so full of sadness that he yearned to spring forward and clasp her in his arms.

He had a passionate desire to learn her troubles and fling himself against them. If only he knew what they were, he felt sure he could conquer them, but it was so dreadfully hard to be kept in the dark like this. It became unbearable at last, and he dashed up to the Rectory, rang the bell, and asked to see Nellie. The lad's excitement was not lost upon Higgins, part of whose business it was to keep his eyes open and his mouth shut. He carried the message to the Doctor, and presently returned with the reply : " Miss Nellie is not at home, sir." These were very dreadful words to Philip, who did not know that they emanated from the Doctor, and was certain that he had seen Nellie at one of the windows.

The only thing to be done was to lay his trouble before Leonard Sterne and ask his advice. And this Philip did.

" Patience, Philip, patience !" said Sterne. " You want to do everything in too much of a hurry. Lucy will soon find out what is the matter; some fancy, no doubt; nothing to be really alarmed at, if only you can manage to persuade the Doctor."

"Oh, dear me, I'll do that. Wait till I have passed my examination and am no longer a pupil. His chief objection to me will then fall to the ground."

"That's true," said Sterne kindly. "But I don't want you to go rushing against some nasty obstacle and coming to grief over it. We could send you to Nice for broken health, or to Boulogne for a broken fortune, but the watering-place that will mend a broken heart has yet to be discovered. *Festina lente*, Philip, is a good maxim in love as well as in everything else."

This conversation occurred on the day preceding that on which Philip was invited to dine at the Rectory. A great dread had been growing upon him that he would have to go away without getting an explanation from Nellie. It would be unendurable, he felt, to go through his examination with some terrible thing hanging over him. But at the Doctor's word he rushed to the other extreme. He was so excited that he could do no more work for the rest of the day. Of course, a dinner-party was not the best place for a private explanation, but then he and Nellie would manage it somehow. What could not love do?

The pace at which he drove the Manor dog-cart that evening called forth many remonstrances from the groom, an old man who had been with the late squire from his boyhood. It was not merely excitement; Philip had spent so much time upon dressing that very little remained for the drive to the Rectory. However, as it happened, he was much more punctual than some of the others who lived close at hand.

When the dog-cart pulled up in front of the clematis-covered porch, the door was immediately opened by Higgins, who stood in the centre of the lamp-light, in a watchful attitude, his white head slightly bowed—the very picture of polished meekness, admirably set among the paintings in the large hall behind him. There was a fresh breeze from the direction of the sea, and Camelback wore a cloudy coronet, but overhead the sky was bright and clear. So Philip told the groom that he would walk back; after which, he was ushered into the drawing-room.

He was conscious of a deeper colour in his cheeks as he advanced to shake hands with Nellie; he knew that he was trembling and felt angry with himself for doing so; he knew also that the others were watching this meeting with the keenest interest. And this knowledge it was that enabled him to get through it as if he were speaking to an ordinary acquaintance. Though a bad hand at anything approaching deception, he was surprised how naturally it came to him. After a few words with the Doctor, who was making himself singularly pleasant to everybody in turn, he slipped away to a quiet corner and began to talk at random to Tattlemaine.

Nellie wore, as Philip afterwards explained to his cousin, " a light blue silk dress, with

some sort of gauzy stuff round the neck." As
a matter of fact, the dress of which this un-
observant young man gave such a miserably
insufficient description, had been specially
made for this very occasion, and cost a sum
that caused the Doctor to pull rather a wry
face. Nellie looked extremely pretty in it,
and not so pale as she would have done in
anything else.

At the same time, Philip was pained to
observe signs, perhaps not of actual ill-health,
but, at any rate, of trouble. The pouting lips
seemed pinched; he could scarcely see a
dimple in the soft cheeks; and once, when
the wondering blue eyes met his, they had
the same sad smile. Still, he knew she loved
him; he saw she was wearing the pearl ring
he had bought for her: it was happiness to
be near her, even if he could not speak to her
yet; and no doubt his chance would come
before it was all over. When the gong
sounded, the Doctor sent Nellie in to dinner
with Viscount Silverspoon, while, as if to
make amends, he playfully took Philip by

the arm, the two bringing up the rear. Philip,
however, scarcely appreciated this arrangement, for it placed him at the farthest possible
distance from Nellie at table. But he could
not help joining in the general merriment,
the Doctor kept up such a constant flow of
anecdotes, chiefly connected with horses.

He was a marvellous old man, this grey-
headed clergyman, tormented day and night
by his anxiety to find that missing son, upon
whom all his hopes rested; forced to ceaseless
activity by the necessity for keeping the
whole of his cumbrous machinery in motion;
and not knowing which way to turn to escape
the heartless scoundrel whose foot was already
upon his neck, and who was daily treading
him lower and lower in the dust. No doubt
his troubles were entirely of his own making,
or, in some cases, his own imagining, but
they were not, on that account, more endur-
able. Sitting at the head of the table, his
tall thin figure as upright as a poplar, his
small sharp-featured face full of pleasant
animation, and his keen little eyes twinkling

with sly fun, the Doctor kept these young
fellows in a continual roar of laughter.
Judging by appearances, it was impossible to
conceive that he had a care in the world; and
yet, at this very moment, the thought would
force itself into his mind, that when these
pupils were gone, he might never be able to
replace them: that the one thing on which
he had set his whole ambition was in imminent
peril.

The dinner was excellent; well chosen,
well cooked, and well served. None of the
guests was afterwards heard to suggest any
improvement; which is saying a good deal,
many of them being confirmed grumblers in
this respect. They even praised the wine,
though here the Doctor had exercised a little
discretion, and had brought out only an
inferior quality, which he thriftily kept for
these occasions. The youthful guests, he
argued, would not know the difference between
good wine and bad; they would believe it to
be precisely what they were told it was; and
this they did, sipping their claret and cham-

pagne with the greatest gusto. They had
been told that he had one of the best cellars
in the county, and fancied that some of it was
now before them. Tattlemaine even went so
far as to compliment the Doctor upon his
claret, and the look in the Doctor's face as
he listened was wonderfully droll.

As soon as Nellie had retired, Silverspoon
made a short speech about the happy days
that he had spent at Puddleton, though he
modestly threw in a doubt as to whether they
might not see him back again. He concluded
by asking them all to drink to the Doctor.

"And an end to his physic," added the
Doctor himself; whereat there was much
laughter. Of course, it was one of his stock
jokes ; unless he had had them cut-and-dry,
he could not possibly have kept the fun
going, when his own mind was so distracted.

When his health had been drunk, he replied
in a light cheery tone at first, but his voice
faltered at the mention of the dear young
friends who were leaving him. As in nearly
everthing that he said and did, there was

some pretence and some sincerity in his words, but at the moment he persuaded himself there was no pretence at all. In conclusion, he proposed the toast of the evening : "The Examiners—' confound their knavish tricks ! ' "

During the wild applause that followed, Higgins entered with cigars and cigarettes, which the Doctor always provided on these occasions, though he himself detested the smell of tobacco smoke.

As the evening wore on, Philip was distressed to find that there was to be no adjournment to the drawing-room, and this became manifest when at length the party broke up. The very fates seemed to be fighting against him. His heart sank like lead at the thought of going away without speaking to Nellie. He had hopefully looked forward to this opportunity, and now it was gone. When he stood with his noisy friends in the hall, he felt supremely miserable.

It was now discovered that a change for the worse had come over the night. The sky was a black mass of wind-driven clouds, and the rain was descending in torrents. This mattered little to those who lived in the village, but Philip, having told the groom not to return for him, had nearly a couple of miles to walk. He was angrily declaring that the man might have had more sense, when the Doctor appeared upon the scene. Philip, he said, must not think of going to the Manor in such a storm of rain; why, he might catch a cold that would utterly spoil his chance of passing his examination; a bed would be ready for him in one of the spare rooms within five minutes, and there he must sleep.

Philip proved very tractable. He was delighted at the thought of spending the night under the same roof as Nellie; her nearness to him must, he felt, sweeten his dreams. Whether it did or not, he saw that his opportunity could scarcely fail to come after all; and thinking that he would rise the first thing in the morning to have it out with Nellie, dear sweet thing that she was, he fell asleep.

CHAPTER IV.

THE EXAMINATION.

It was nearly eight o'clock when Philip stole quietly downstairs. His excitement had brought on a reaction; he felt a sense of depression which was increased by the quietude and strangeness of the house, and also by the rain that was still pouring heavily without. The pictured hall wore quite a different aspect in the cold grey light, while the wind whistled around the porch as if it were determined to get in.

Higgins, who was carefully brushing the Doctor's hat, put it down when Philip appeared, and advanced to wish him a polite good morning. Standing in an attitude of respectful attention, he suggested that the study would be the most comfortable room to

wait in ; and thither Philip went, merely to
get rid of him. When he found that Nellie
was not there, he very soon dodged into the
drawing-room. Wishing to surprise her, he
walked as stealthily as Mr. Valentine Gaunt,
but the eager look died out of his bright
young face as soon as he discovered the room
to be empty. Perhaps she was in the conservatory. He advanced on tiptoe and peeped
in. Yes. There she was, looking as sweet
and fair as the rosebud over which she was
bending.

"Nellie," he said softly.

"Philip," she exclaimed, starting and
blushing.

"Yes, it's me, Nellie. Are you glad to see
me ? "

"Yes and No, Philip," she replied, stealing
a sad shy glance at him' over the tiny hand
which she had raised to her mouth as if to
guard some secret.

After a stare of pained bewilderment, he
started forward with outstretched hands,
saying, "Darling, what does it all mean ? "

"I don't know who I am," she replied, shrinking away from him. "Don't touch me; please don't—don't."

"Don't—know—who—you—are!"

"There, Philip, I didn't mean to say that. This is a dreary world, full of trouble and misery. But perhaps it will all come right; you always say it will. Oh, Philip, do you really think it will?"

"Surely, my pet, surely. Why, dear me, what are trees meant for but to cut down? And what are troubles?"

"Well, I hope so," she interrupted, plucking nervously at the rosebud. "But you must go away now."

"Go away now!" He could only echo the dreadful words. A shiver passed through him as he stood there blankly staring at her.

"Nellie," he faltered presently, "I am going away to-day—up to London—for my examination—and I shan't be back for three weeks, and there is no knowing what may happen in three weeks—or in a railway journey."

The shapely head with its masses of dark hair was bent down, and the face that he loved to look upon was turned away from him. He could see a tremulous swaying of the slender figure, but he had no suspicion that Nellie was sobbing.

After a pause there came a faint : " Bless you, my Philip."

" Is that all ? " he asked reproachfully. And then a sudden fury seized upon him. His hands were clenched, and his tones fierce, as he cried, " Has that man Gaunt done this thing ? If he has—— "

But here the Doctor dashed into the drawing-room ; so they both had to compose their faces and go out to meet him. Doubtless, Higgins had told him that they were together in the conservatory, but he showed not the smallest sign of displeasure. That was not his way at all ; he loved to circumvent, but he saw no good in knocking his head against accomplished facts and making himself and everybody else uncomfortable to no purpose. He kissed Nellie very tenderly, and shook hands with Philip; and in a few minutes the young people were surprised to find themselves laughing. The weather never seemed to make any impression on the Doctor's iron frame. He was very nearly as cheerful at breakfast as he had been at dinner on the previous night, and his good spirits were so hearty and so contagious, that it was not until Philip was on his way to the Manor, without having had any explanation from Nellie, that he began to feel astonished at himself.

It was an exciting and, to some extent, a melancholy day in Puddleton. There was very little work done, for those who were left behind wanted to see how their friends looked on the eve of taking a frightful leap across or into the Rubicon, maliciously set in their path by those desperadoes, the Civil Service Examiners.

While each vehicle was being piled with luggage, a huge amount in many cases, an anxious group stood around; and when it drove off through the street of creeper-clad cottages, with here and there a smock-frocked labourer hoeing in his little garden, and Camelback peering out of the mist, there was always a ringing cheer. The weather was still very gloomy, but the rain having cleared off, nearly everybody was out of doors. Heavisides went to bid each of his departing friends good-bye, and as he walked, he smoked his pipe and strummed placidly on his banjo. But his smile was a little troubled, and he gazed with embarrassing earnestness at every one who was considered likely to be successful, as if he would thus discover the way it should be done.

The last to drive through the village was Philip Strathclyde. They gave him a hearty cheer, and so he, too, went on his way, Puddleton being left in a temporary state of despondency.

Most of the Doctor's candidates went to their own homes in London. For the others, the whole of one house—a lodging-house in a quiet street near the scene of operations—had been engaged and placed in charge of

Mr. Jostler, who led a particularly anxious three weeks there. Still, he got a certain amount of enjoyment out of it. More than once he announced that he had a small suggestion to offer, but as he never succeeded in getting to the end of it, no one knew what it was about. That he realized the importance of his position, there can be no doubt, for he spent most of his time in walking about the rooms, stroking his long beard, and, when the opportunity occurred, making speeches to the candidates who had just returned for meals from Burlington House, and were clamorous to learn whether their answers were correct.

Philip was one of those under Mr. Jostler's charge, but he certainly gave no trouble, for he was too bent upon passing his examination to do anything but work—very nervously at first, but with more confidence afterwards. The first few papers he " floored " in grand style, according to his own account. He answered every word of the French grammar, not without an uneasy feeling of surprise. But when it came to the French translation, a glance at the paper brought an angry flush to his cheeks; he hastily rose from his seat and strode out of the room. So far as Philip Strathclyde was concerned, the examination was at an end.

The others, who had often enviously watched his pen flying across the paper, looked after him with amazement. It was the most startling collapse they had ever witnessed. Surely he had not found himself unable to scramble through the translation somehow! It certainly was difficult; at least, such was the opinion of Plantagenet and Silverspoon as they hurried back to question Philip.

"I couldn't make head or tail of some parts," observed Plantagenet, with a puzzled look. "What the deuce is the meaning of 'preoccupied graves'? Some allusion to body-snatching, I suppose; but I'm hanged if I could make it fit in neatly."

"Preoccupied graves!" exclaimed Silverspoon. "What was the French?"

"Here it is," replied Plantagenet, producing the paper, "*Des graves préoccupations.*"

"I thought that was 'grave preoccupations.'"

"But what's the meaning of that?"

"Goodness knows, but I'm sure it's right."

"Hang it all!" cried Plantagenet. "Then I'm ploughed for a moral."

When Silverspoon had finished laughing at his friend, he asked: "But what did you make of that odd passage about a race between the Atlantic and a hippopotamus?"

"A what?" demanded Plantagenet, in some astonishment.

"A race between the Atlantic and a hippopotamus, but I'm not quite certain about the hippopotamus."

"Turn it up and let us have a look at it."

Silverspoon pointed to the words, "*La course entre Atalante et Hippomène.*" Plantagenet stopped in the street to roar with laughter.

"Why," he explained at length, "don't you remember Sterne telling us about a fellow who ran a race with a girl, and won by chucking apples at her? Well, he was called Hippomenes and she Atalanta."

"Confound it! I suppose I'm ploughed too," said Silverspoon. "I call it a scandalous shame to shove classics into a French paper."

These words brought the unfortunate couple to the door of Mr. Jostler's temporary abode.

They found Philip standing at the drawing-room window, looking dismally at the monotonous row of houses opposite, with a hansom crawling along the street, and a piano-organ performing in the gutter for the benefit of a solitary shoe-black; not a very cheery prospect. Philip turned round to ask his friends how they had got on, but he refused to answer any questions about himself. His behaviour struck them as very singular. They were inclined to wonder whether, as the Doctor had feared, he had not overworked himself, and so become a little queer in the head. "Probably," he said, " they would know all in time, but he could not explain his reasons at present." And with this they were obliged to be content.

Being now a gentleman at large, Philip felt at liberty to amuse himself. He went that evening to the Parnassus and sat in the front row of the stalls. The theatre was badly ventilated and the piece uninteresting, otherwise Philip would not have got such a good seat. The result was that though he did not actually fall asleep, he became very drowsy.

Presently he was startled at hearing a voice that sounded strangely familiar to his ears. He felt sure that it was Arnold Copingstone's. Fancying that he must have been dreaming, he rubbed his eyes and stared at the stage, which was occupied by a family party and a footman. Had he seen the latter before he had heard him, he might have had some difficulty in recognizing Nellie's brother in the liveried flunkey with powdered hair, but those drawling tones set all doubt at rest.

It was an astounding discovery, for Philip had supposed Arnold to be at Oxford. It was also a very dreadful discovery in many ways. Naturally enough, it affected Philip most keenly, in so far as it concerned his and Nellie's prospects. He saw that it had placed a terrible obstacle before them, and guessed that the Doctor was already aware of it, which would account for his opposition to their marriage. It was the Doctor's ambition, he knew, to build up a mighty establishment which should endure generation after generation; but how could this be done now? There was only one way, and that a poor one; by the marriage of Nellie to some able tutor, who would undertake the management.

Philip, as we know, was partly right and partly wrong in his conclusion. Though the Doctor had long been acquainted with Arnold's disappearance, he had no idea as to what had become of him, and still continued his efforts for finding him. He clung desperately to the hope of putting matters back in the old groove before it was discovered they had departed from it. When the time came for him to learn that this could never be, then indeed it would go hard with him.

At the conclusion of the performance, Philip asked his way to the stage-door, and there he met Arnold, who greeted him as if their meeting were a matter of course, and contained no element out of the common.

He spoke to Philip as if they had only just parted from one another. This, more than anything else, tended to bring Philip back to a calmer frame of mind.

Very little in the way of explanation was said in the street, which was full of bustle and noise. But, at Philip's suggestion, they went off together to a neighbouring restaurant, and had supper in a brilliantly-lighted room on the first floor, with mirrors all round the walls, and different couples sitting at the little tables. The two friends occupied a table in a corner near one of the windows.

After having exacted a pledge of secrecy, Arnold narrated his adventures since leaving Puddleton. There were only three things that he omitted to mention : his theatrical *nom-de-guerre*, which it never occurred to Philip was other than Copingstone; his present address, which Philip never thought of asking for, since Arnold was always to be found at the Parnassus; and his meeting with Mr. Valentine Gaunt. He concluded with an amusing account of M. Dubarri.

Philip tried hard to induce him to communicate with the Doctor, but without the slightest effect. No, he replied, he would not do that until he had attained complete independence.

" Then," said Philip, earnestly, " mayn't I tell Nellie ? "

" A woman ! " said Arnold, raising his eyes to reflect the smile that he saw in his friend's face.

"Not yet," put in Philip, in extenuation of Nellie's crime.

" How old is she ? " asked the brother.

" Nineteen ; and before she is twenty she will be my wife—I hope," added he, suddenly remembering this last difficulty.

" Is that matter for congratulation ? "

" You old humbug, Arnold ! When you and Hebe are tied up in a bundle, see if I don't chaff you."

" It's not a thing to joke about, I can tell you. When that bundle, as you call it, is tossing along the matrimonial billows, it must sink if we can't swim together, for we shall be tied up too closely to be able to swim separately. Marriage is a very awful thing, Philip. Upon my word, when a fellow comes to look at it seriously—— "

" Which you never did in your life. But really, Arnold, may I tell Nellie ? She is so terribly anxious. Just a word, at any rate, to say that you are safe and well."

" Will you guarantee that she keeps my secret ? "

" From her father ? " exclaimed Philip, who felt sure that he would never get Nellie to make any such promise, and now bitterly repented having tied himself down.

" I'll tell you what I'll do, Philip," said Arnold, dropping the knife he had been playing with; "I'll write to her. Will that satisfy you?"

"Yes, if you do it at once; this very night."

Of course, Philip knew he was hastening the very thing that he dreaded, but then he had Nellie's happiness to consider, to say nothing of the Doctor's. Besides, he could not bear the idea of continually facing a terrible uncertainty. He wanted to know what he had to meet, and so to prepare for it. Even if it cut Nellie and her father deeply, it would be far better to have it over and done with as soon as possible.

Philip returned to Puddleton on the following day. Some unfortunates had already arrived there, and others kept dropping in during the week. It is scarcely necessary to say that Plantagenet and Silverspoon were among the number; so also were Merridale and Tattlemaine. They met with very scanty commiseration from the other pupils, who were indeed inclined to laugh at each arrival. Heavisides smilingly strummed them back upon his banjo, just as he had strummed them away.

It soon became evident that Puddleton had fared very badly in the examination, and it was afterwards discovered that most of the failures were due to low marks in classics. The cause, no doubt, was the disorderly conduct that had been prevalent at one time, and also the accident of an unusually stiff paper. It was certainly no fault of Sterne's, yet he felt it keenly.

Mr. Valentine Gaunt spoke very strongly on the matter. It was his opportunity, and he was not likely to let it slip. It was exceedingly hard, he said, that the labour of all the other tutors should be wasted through the incompetence of one; he really wondered how the Doctor could be so foolish as to keep a man so evidently incapable. This was a very pleasant doctrine to those who had failed. They were glad enough to lay the blame on some one else's shoulders, and here it was done for them.

Of course this only added to the Doctor's

distress and uneasiness. That he, after having been so wonderfully successful, should be in danger of losing his pupils through repeated failures, was a new source of alarm. He summoned a cabinet council to consider the situation.

It was with unusually solemn faces that the Professors assembled in the study. Among the group standing in the bow-window which looked out upon the tennis-court, with its fencing of laurels, was Leonard Sterne. His long face was grave and anxious, but it also contained another expression that attracted many curious glances. He seldom spoke, and when he did, there was in his voice a strange quiver, suggesting a severe mental strain. Mr. Jostler, who was clearly lubricating something, fondled his big beard near the tiled grate behind the Doctor's chair, and most of the others were standing or sitting in front of the bookcase opposite. Mr. Valentine Gaunt, who arrived rather late, hovered stealthily to a seat at the Doctor's right hand, and sat down with folded arms.

With the arrangements for screwing up the machinery to a higher state of efficiency, we have no concern. The Doctor was an adept in matters of the sort, and in the present case seemed fairly well satisfied. He had just expressed himself to this effect, when Mr. Jostler stepped forward and said—

"Might I suggest, Dr. Copingstone——"

"No, no," exclaimed the Doctor hurriedly. "Pray don't, Mr. Jostler, pray don't."

Mr. Jostler retired, looking round for sympathy. If he had been content to drop preliminaries, and give his speech by instalments, he might have eased himself of it long ago, but the unfortunate man would insist upon its wholesale delivery.

While this incident was in progress, Sterne advanced to the side of the writing-table opposite Mr. Valentine Gaunt, and stood there with his knuckles resting upon it. His face made it very clear that something unusual was about to occur. He looked steadfastly at the Doctor, who had thrown himself back in his chair, and, while his fingers played uneasily with his grey hair, was regarding his lieutenant with evident apprehension.

"Dr. Copingstone," Sterne said firmly, yet in tones that had a hard nervous ring, "there is one thing connected with the examination that needs explanation. It is a most unpleasant subject, but as it concerns the honour of all in this room, and also of the pupils, I feel it must be gone into."

Sterne paused, as if for breath. The silence was profound, every one gazing at him with the greatest anxiety, to learn what was coming next. Instinctively one or two glanced at Mr. Valentine Gaunt, who was still sitting with folded arms. There was a glitter in his eyes that boded mischief.

"Go on, Sterne," said the Doctor hoarsely. Such was the tension of his feelings that he unconsciously dropped the prefix which he invariably used when anybody else was present.

"With one significant exception," resumed Sterne, with a little gasp—"I'll refer to it presently, if necessary—all our candidates at the Civil Service Examinations have been lately getting very high marks in French, whereas those we have sent up to the Universities, and elsewhere, have got very low ones. It is a remarkable contrast. Perhaps Mr. Gaunt, if only for his own sake, will explain it."

All eyes were now withdrawn from Sterne and fixed upon his rival, who still made no movement, and so they went backwards and forwards the whole time.

"Is Mr. Sterne jealous of my success?" asked Mr. Valentine Gaunt, with an angry little laugh. "He is always telling us that he has only the interests of the pupils at heart; surely he is not going to reproach me for getting them high marks in French to counterbalance the low marks in Latin and Greek! By working together, we have managed to urge the coach forward, and bring some, at any rate, to their destination."

"The floy on the wheel's a wasp," was the whispered comment of Mr. O'Shee, Professor of Geography.

"Then," said Sterne, "does Mr. Gaunt's explanation consist merely of an attack upon me? I ask, because I should like it to come from him, and not from anybody else."

"So far, I see nothing to explain," said Mr. Valentine Gaunt, with a supercilious smile. "My duty here is to knock English and French into the heads of the pupils committed to my charge. It is for the examiners, and not me, to get it out. If they succeed in some cases, and fail in others, I can scarcely be held responsible, though it suits Mr. Sterne, whose own method is very deplorable, to think so."

Sterne looked more distressed than indignant. He hesitated a few moments, and then spoke with difficulty.

"Well," he said, with a sigh, "I am now compelled to return to the significant exception I mentioned. I mean Philip Strathclyde. He did not get a single mark for French translation. Can Mr. Gaunt tell us why?"

"Probably, when no longer under Mr. Sterne's almost parental supervision, his young friend indulged in a little relaxation, instead of presenting himself for examination."

"Need I contradict that, Dr. Coping-stone ? "

" I have every confidence in Philip Strath-clyde," remarked the Doctor, notwithstand-ing his reluctance to be dragged into a dispute in the same way that he often dragged others.

" And so have I," added Sterne, with great earnestness. " He is a noble-minded young fellow, and few would have done what he did. He refused to send in a French transla-tion paper. Can Mr. Gaunt tell us why ?"

" No, I can't," replied Mr. Valentine Gaunt sharply.

He had unfolded his arms, and was tugging viciously at his whiskers. He tried to look indifferent, but the tell-tale spots on his cheekbones had begun to glow, and his heavy brows were ominously contracted.

" Must I still go on ? "

" Oh, by all means. You are deliciously mysterious."

" Philip Strathclyde acted as he did because he wouldn't take an unfair advantage of the other candidates. He was at first delighted, and afterwards surprised, to find that he had been specially prepared in nearly every question in the grammar paper ; but when it came to the pieces set for translation, and he saw that these also he had done with Mr. Gaunt, he could come to only one conclusion."

Mr. Valentine Gaunt sprang to his feet.

" And what is that, Mr. Sterne ? " he loudly demanded, with an angry gesture.

" Perhaps you can answer the question better than I can."

" Am I accused of having seen the paper beforehand ? "

Alas ! his method usually followed his temper.

" You are your own accuser," said Sterne severely.

Every one expected a very violent scene to ensue, Mr. Valentine Gaunt's attitude was so threatening. The Doctor, with a pitiably troubled expression, half rose to prevent an accident, but dropped back in his chair again. The others held their breath, as they watched these two staring at one another across the writing-table.

However, Mr. Valentine Gaunt saw his mistake, and quickly recovered himself.

"I once asked you for an explanation, Mr. Sterne," he said in his harshest tones, "and you refused to give it to me. I claim the same privilege now. If the Doctor thinks there is anything to explain, I am quite ready to explain to him, and to him alone. I acknowledge no other authority."

"If you satisfy him," said Sterne, "you will satisfy me, and, I think I can say, all of us; but the honour of the place certainly demands an explanation."

"Dr. Copingstone," said Mr. Jostler, solemnly stroking his beard as he came forward.

"Well," said the Doctor, without thinking.

Here was the long-wished-for opportunity come at last. Smiling with satisfaction, Mr. Jostler threw himself into an important attitude, and was about to begin, when the Doctor happened to look round. His face became the very picture of dismay.

"Bless the man, I declare he's going to make a speech," said the Doctor. And before the others could interchange smiles, he was literally running from the room, glad enough, no doubt, to put an end to a very painful situation.

Mr. Jostler was not to be baulked this time, however. He was far too uneasy to retain his speech any longer; and, though the Professors at once began to disperse, he nevertheless kept on unreeling his supreme effort. Higgins, who was rather a wag, declared that when he peeped into the study an hour later, he found Mr. Jostler still speaking—to empty benches.

The result of the foregoing incident was to split up the tutors into two sections, and to develop among them the strong party spirit that had long been rife among the pupils.

It might be supposed that they would gather round Sterne, but, as a matter of fact, only a

few did. Except where the Doctor was concerned, he was far too rigid to be generally
popular among his colleagues, who could not
forget his share in the dismissal of the unfortunate Jenkins. It was not, of course, to
his having his own ideas of right and wrong
that they objected; it was to *their* being tried
by his hard-and-fast rule, which never admitted of extenuating circumstances. They
were good fellows for the most part, but they
thought Sterne angular, and could not get on
with him.

It was different with Mr. Valentine Gaunt,
whose method largely consisted in making
himself popular, and whose morality was not
too severe. None of them stood in his way,
so he was very friendly with all. Feeling
that his position was too well established for
there to be any need to assert it in their case,
he ran no risk of giving offence, but treated
each as his equal. He reaped the benefit of
his self-restraint now.

The balance leaned unmistakably against
Leonard Sterne. The majority of his col-

leagues, with a little natural bias, decided that he had given way to jealous suspicions which had no foundation. Mr. Valentine Gaunt had made a lucky *coup* in respect to the French papers, and the instinct of self-preservation had caused Sterne to turn against him. This was his own explanation, and it was generally accepted. What other was possible? Sterne could not disprove it, and, therefore, had no right to deny it; he was obliged to give it his tacit adhesion; and his silence was construed against him.

For his own part, he had resolved to hold his hand for the present. After all, he might be a prejudiced judge of what had happened. He would wait until the next examination, and then, if the same thing happened again, insist upon Mr. Valentine Gaunt's dismissal, or leave Puddleton himself.

In the acrimonious disputes that ensued between the two factions, Puddleton threatened to go to pieces. It was noticeable that many of those who stoutly defended Sterne, nevertheless shunned his company, as if they were either ashamed of him or afraid of his powerful rival. He was not slow to perceive his growing isolation, and felt it deeply.

"The Doctor would help me if he could," he sadly said to his wife, one afternoon shortly after the meeting at the Rectory, "but I can see he is powerless. I don't know why, yet there is the fact. If it were not for that, I should leave the place as soon as possible. But we can't desert our friend, whatever happens."

"I think the Doctor is a very poor friend, Leonard," said his wife, who was sitting opposite him in the study, "and a very weak man, too."

"Only where his ambition is touched, Lucy. He is strong enough in all else."

"At any rate, I don't see why you should help him if he won't help you. I do like fair play. It's simply dreadful, your wearing yourself out day and night, while——" She broke off to say in answer to a knock at the door, "Come in. Well, Jane, what is it now?"

' " If you please, ma'am," replied the servant, " Miss Nellie is in the drawing-room, and she particularly wishes to see you alone."

Mrs. Sterne rose and went downstairs.

CHAPTER V

THE register in the family Bible did not contain Nellie's name. This was the trouble that she now confided to her friend, Mrs. Sterne. Was she an orphan, she tremblingly asked, whom, in the goodness of his heart, the Doctor had adopted ? Who was she, and what was she ? What was her name ?

The two were sitting side by side in the drawing-room at the Hut, an artistically-furnished room, looking out upon the street of straggling old-fashioned houses, now scarcely visible for the tide of greenery that was surging over them in the warm sunlight.

" Oh, what a silly puss it is, to be sure ! " said Lucy Sterne, tenderly stroking Nellie's dark hair. " Of course it is a mistake. Your father has forgotten to enter your name ; that's all, Nellie."

" But he has entered my poor darling mother's death. If he had forgotten my birth before, surely he would have remembered it then."

" At such a time, dear, he wouldn't be likely to remember anything."

" Then why did he hide the Bible away from me ? " asked Nellie, sadly shaking her head. " Why did he say the keys of the bookcase were lost, when they are not ? "

" Why, Nellie, you yourself have often told me that there is only one key."

" And so there is ; but it fits all the three doors, and I can't see how there could ever have been another. He said the keys were lost long before my mother was taken from us, and yet there it is all written down."

" Perhaps, in his grief, he may have gone mechanically to the bookcase and used the one key," suggested kind-hearted Mrs. Sterne, at her wits' end for some scrap of comfort,

" and have forgotten how he did it, afterwards. I have heard of such things, Nellie."

In spite of her cheerful face, she felt sorely troubled, for she had not her husband's faith in the Doctor. On the contrary, she gave him little credit for good motives, but, judging him by the tricks that he was continually playing, was inclined to consider him an unscrupulous man whose winning manner formed part of his stock-in-trade : a verdict prompted chiefly by her resentment against the Doctor for his treatment of her husband, whose meekness scarcely met with her approval. There was a limit, she felt, even to Christian endurance ; and if she had been allowed, she would many a time have gone boldly to the Doctor and have given him a piece of her mind, regardless of the fact that she was ignorant of his position. Indeed, she had more than once thrown out such an unmistakable hint that he was almost as much afraid of her as of Mr. Jostler.

Her distrust of him led her to ask permission to lay the matter before her husband,

and, after receiving a promise that it should
go no farther, Nellie reluctantly consented.
She left shortly afterwards, feeling much
happier for Mrs. Sterne's assurance that she
would put everything right; in what way she
forgot to explain.

Leonard Sterne listened to his wife's story
in silence, watching her intently, as if the
formation as well as the sound of the words
were of the utmost importance. While she
went chattering on, he sat stiffly in his chair,
his body bent rather forward, and his face
devoid of any other expression than concen-
trated attention. When she finished speaking,
he said merely—

"Nellie should have gone straight to her
father instead of coming to us."

"That may be, Leonard," replied his wife,
with a sense of disappointment at the prospect
of having to stand aloof from an attractive
mystery; "but the Doctor has never treated
his children as he does anybody else, and if
they take their secrets elsewhere, it is his
own fault. Besides, I think Nellie is quite

right. She is a dear good girl, and she
doesn't want to pain him needlessly. Now
that her mind has been disturbed, she must
be told the truth, whatever it is; and it would
be far better if she could be reassured without
letting the Doctor suspect the disquieting
thoughts that must be passing through her
poor head. That's her opinion, at any rate,
and it is mine, too."

"I see," he remarked, with a grave smile,
"you are both pupils of the Doctor."

"Thank you for nothing, Leonard. But
will you help Nellie or won't you?"

"Do you mean by speaking to the
Doctor?"

"No, she won't allow that, and she won't
speak to him herself."

"You must give me time to think it over,
Lucy," he said, taking up his pen.

"But can't you suggest any explanation?"
she asked, curiously.

"Perhaps the entry of Mrs. Copingstone's
death was made by Arnold. The Doctor,
forgetting about the missing keys, might

have asked him to perform what would be an exceptionally painful task for a husband. You often say, Lucy, he is fond of shifting his burdens on to the shoulders of others."

" But you never agree with me."

" Well, I'll do so now. Father and son write very much alike; and if Arnold has found out a way of opening the bookcase, he is just the sort of fellow never to mention it."

" Hem ! " said Lucy Sterne, and took up her work. Presently she looked up to ask, " Will you write to Arnold ? "

Nellie had received and shown her father a letter from her brother, giving neither address nor any particulars about himself except that he was safe and well. But she was still strictly forbidden to say anything likely to lead people to suppose that he was not at Oxford.

" I'll see," answered Leonard Sterne, lighting his pipe, and puffing away vigorously. He remembered, among other things, the

picture of "the Old Adam," and felt it better
to drop the subject until he had thoroughly
turned it over in his mind.

If he could have relied upon the Doctor to
tell "the truth, the whole truth, and nothing
but the truth," his course would have been
plain enough; but in all probability, if he
were to ask for an explanation, he would
merely have dust thrown in his eyes. It was
an embarrassing position, perhaps the most
embarrassing that a man can be placed in.
He had the firmest faith in the Doctor's ends,
but detested his tricky means; he earnestly
desired to help his friend, but could not
implicitly trust him.

The more he reflected, the more strongly
he felt that he dared not advise Nellie to lay
the matter before her father at present; it
might only provoke him into telling her one
of his well-intentioned "white lies," and this
Sterne could not reconcile with his conscience.
Moreover, he could not even guess what rocks .
might be lying ahead, and to send her blind-
fold into unknown dangers would have been

the grossest cruelty. No, he decided that he must act himself. But how?

Sterne's difficulty was this: he did not know whether to gather up the various clues into a single skein, or which, if they were all separate, he ought to follow. It seemed impossible that there could be any connection between Mr. Valentine Gaunt's influence over the Doctor, and the singular omission from the family Bible; and, as if the affair were not sufficiently complicated, there were several other circumstances which he could not fit in with either.

While he was still trying to piece this puzzle, though pretending to be engaged in looking over Gammon's accounts, Philip Strathclyde entered the room. He was warmly greeted by Sterne and his wife, and sat down by the latter's side on the couch in the window.

Philip had been a good deal cut up by the sickness that comes from " hope deferred," but his cheerful disposition had already enabled him to leave it behind. In a few

more months there would be another examination, and then all would be well. To
prevent the chance of another accident, he
had insisted upon being transferred from
Mr. Valentine Gaunt's classes to Mr. Jostler's,
who also taught French and English; for the
Doctor still had two tutors for each subject,
and played the one against the other. He
saw the many little advantages of this rivalry,
but was not even yet keenly alive to the one
big disadvantage, though it was threatening
to bring the place about his ears.

"Do you think the Doctor was aware of
Mr. Gaunt's foreknowledge of the French
papers?" asked Philip, in his outspoken way.

"Certainly not, Philip," returned Sterne
hotly. "I am surprised that you should ask
such a thing."

"Well, I'm rather surprised at myself, but
so many astonishing things have occurred
lately that I don't know what to think."

"That's no reason, my friend, why you
should bring a monstrous charge against the
Doctor."

" He has only himself to blame for any charges that are brought against him," said Mrs. Sterne. " What has put this idea into your head, Mr. Strathclyde ? "

" It would explain so many things," replied Philip, thinking of the explanation itself rather than of the serious accusation involved in it. " Why he had engaged for an important post a man who had, I'm certain, never held a tutorship before, and why that man had afterwards turned round upon him."

Mrs. Sterne looked at her husband with a triumphant little smile, but the moment she caught sight of his troubled face, she turned to Philip and said stoutly—

" No, Mr. Strathclyde, you are quite wrong. The Doctor is worried about Mr. Gaunt, but, be assured, for a totally different reason. Some of his ways "—she was quoting her husband's opinion—" may not be in accordance with our notions, but he has a kind good heart, which is the main thing, after all. Don't you think so, Leonard ? "

He gave her a grateful look as he replied,

" Yes, decidedly. You are young and impulsive, Philip, and don't mean any harm, I
know. But I would strongly warn you
against jumping at a hurtful theory because
it seems plausible. Look a little deeper, and
then see what becomes of your suggestion.
If the Doctor had really been engaged in
these infamous transactions, he would naturally
have tried to get the greatest benefit from
them ; in which case, Mr. Jostler would not
have a single pupil in French—they would
all be taught by Mr. Gaunt. This disposes
of your theory at once. But, in my opinion,
the matter is altogether beyond the region of
argument. The Doctor is your friend and
mine, and, therefore, we should believe only
what is good of him."

" I'll try to do so," said Philip, penitently,
" and I'm exceedingly sorry that I said anything to vex you. I'm always putting my
foot in it."

" Oh, that's all right, Philip," returned
Sterne, kindly. " I can quite understand
your anxiety to set up a known obstacle in

the place of an unknown danger, so as to
have the satisfaction of demolishing it; but
then, you see, one runs the risk of demolishing
the wrong thing. And now I have some news
to tell you. I said that sooner or later Mrs.
Sterne would find out what was the matter
with Nellie, and she has done so to-day."

"Oh, Mrs. Sterne, I don't know how to
thank you enough," exclaimed Philip.

"I can't take any credit," he said. "I
have asked Nellie several times, but she
never would tell me until this afternoon,
when she came to me of her own accord."

"And what is it?"

"Nothing very serious, I think," answered
Sterne, "but I can't tell you yet, if I would;
and, what's more, I think it better for you
not to know at present. I am still of opinion
that if you can persuade the Doctor, all will
be well."

"Oh, dear me, I'll do that," said Philip,
with a confident smile. "The last examination was a very terrible thing, of course, but
next time——" He stopped, and his face

became very grave, for he suddenly recollected the disquieting change that had taken place in the situation.

It was hard for Philip that he could not take counsel with Leonard Sterne about the alarming prospect opened up by the discovery of Arnold in London. For all he knew, it might be the very thing that was making Nellie avoid him, and causing her father such evident anxiety, and yet he was powerless to help either. Philip felt bound in honour to his friend; like many young fellows, he held that his word once given could never be retracted—not even for the purpose of averting disaster. In fact, his opinion on this point was the opposite extreme to the Doctor's.

Philip, as we have seen, was ready enough to look at the darker side of the picture; not with the object of groaning at it and calling others to groan at it, as many do; but in order to find out some way of turning it round. Such difficulties as he had to encounter, he preferred to meet on his own ground. Hence the necessity for immediate action pressed heavily upon him now. Supposing the fact of Arnold's having gone on the stage to be unknown to Mr. Valentine Gaunt, he had no idea that the methodical man had already fitted it in with his own plans, but he was sharp enough to perceive that it was well adapted to that purpose. This, he felt, would be nothing short of a catastrophe for all his friends. His uneasiness was increased by Sterne's vague words about Nellie, for he was in such a state of muddle that he strung everything upon the same thread. He decided to seek an immediate interview with Arnold, who held the key of the position.

He told Sterne he was going to London, but nothing more. Then he walked to the Rectory. While he was following the grave but watchful Higgins through the hall, he heard Mr. Valentine Gaunt's voice in the drawing-room. It gave him a shock as if he had inadvertently entered a shower-bath. His face turned a bright crimson, for this fair-haired lad had the delicate skin that

colours with painful ease, and he clenched
his fist in the attempt to control his anger.
The fellow was always dangling about Nellie ;
if he should dare to—— But never mind ;
his flank was about to be turned by a movement that he little suspected. Philip had
some wild idea of bringing Arnold back to
Puddleton, if absolutely necessary, by the
coat-collar : anything, rather than that they
should go sliding over the precipice that was
gaping before them.

His request for a couple of days' leave of
absence was at once granted by the Doctor,
who inquired what he was going to do in
London, but merely for the sake of something
to say. Philip turned the question aside.
He was equally reticent with his aunt, and
wore quite an important air of mystery.

The same evening he arrived in London,
and, after a hasty dinner, proceeded to the
Parnassus, where a grievous disappointment
awaited him. Arnold had left the theatre,
and, so far as Philip could learn, his address
was unknown there.

CHAPTER VI.

AN UNPLEASANT SURPRISE.

Iт has been hinted that the piece in which Arnold played the part of footman was not a financial success. Within a week of his unexpected meeting with Philip, it collapsed. A new piece was immediately substituted for it, but the new "cast" did not contain the name of that rising young actor, Arnold Cressingham. M. Dubarri wrung his hands in despair, and then clenched and shook them in violent indignation; he declaimed against the stupidity of theatrical managers; but he ended by cheering up and exhorting his pupil to cheer up.

"Pscha! it is nothing—nothing," he said, patting Arnold affectionately on the shoulder.

" He is a donkey, that fellow Footlight, who doesn't know his own business. See, he fails! There is the proof of what I say to you. Never fear, my friend with the grand passion, you will soon get another engagement; and after, you will make a fortune."

Arnold was beginning to feel a little doubtful on this point. He had an uncomfortable suspicion that his last engagement was due to his calves and his figure generally; which, if true, did not hold out a very strong hope of his ever taking high rank in his profession. He cheered up, of course; that is to say, he showed no outward signs of despondency; but he could not help thinking occasionally of the time—a time very close at hand—when his money would be exhausted.

M. Dubarri, who had lost his old pupils by changing his address, and had not yet succeeded in getting any new ones, had already begun to husband their common resources. The bottle of claret was rarely seen on the table, and though he still brought in little delicacies for supper with the same delightful air of mystery, they were always of a cheaper sort than hitherto. In short, he did his utmost to forget his own troubles, and to make Arnold forget his, with such success that no one would have guessed the extremities to which the small household was often driven for the sake of appearances.

M. Dubarri even found some comfort in the termination of Arnold's connection with the Parnassus. He laboured under the dread that London was pervaded by emissaries of Mr. Valentine Gaunt, and insisted upon Arnold's taking extraordinary precautions against being followed home from the theatre. These precautions had latterly been abandoned; chiefly, it must be said, because Arnold saw no need of them any longer, and was too indolent to put them into practice. But as for M. Dubarri, if he was only going as far as the public-house at the corner, he always proceeded in a very wily manner, making wild dashes from one safe spot to another, and generally behaving in a way that had induced more than one detective to set off in pursuit.

All this afforded a good deal of amusement to Arnold, who, in his search for a fresh engagement, invariably selected the shortest road, and pursued it without heed to the passers-by.

One fine afternoon early in June, when returning from one of these expeditions, he was strolling along Parnassus Street—a neighbourhood that M. Dubarri had implored him to shun, or, at any rate, to be particularly careful in passing through. It was a noisy, bustling thoroughfare, full of hurrying people whose footsteps were scarcely audible amid the continuous roar of heavy traffic. Looking neither to the right nor to the left, Arnold, as usual, walked straight ahead, his tall stalwart figure seeming to cleave a way through the crowd. But at the hair-dresser's shop which he had frequented since his connection with the neighbouring theatre, he stopped; and, after a slight hesitation, disappeared through the door.

There were two men lounging near the lamp-post on the opposite side of the street. At the sight of Arnold, one of them started, and began to stare. Then he whispered a few words to the other, who hurried away, and was soon lost among the crowd.

Meanwhile, Arnold had entered the shop. There were no other customers in it at the time, only the proprietress herself and the smart young damsel with frizzled hair and the black eyes who had smiled so boldly at the parson in a tasselled hat. Madame Farnienti was a plump, good-looking woman, with very pale blue eyes and very light flaxen hair, and perhaps a slightly vixenish expression. She was fashionably dressed, except that she wore rather more jewellery than is usual in the daytime.

She and her assistant were looking over a book that resembled a ledger. When Arnold entered, she pushed it away with an exclamation of impatience, saying—

"I do wish I could get hold of that long-bearded parson in the tasselled hat. Mr.

Valentine Gaunt, the private gentleman, I suppose ! ' "

" Leonard Sterne," said Arnold, thinking aloud.

"Eh ? what, sir ? " she demanded sharply.

" Hair-cutting," replied Arnold, and passed into the back shop. He had no wish to give a possible clue to his own identification and discovery.

It was a puzzling incident, which gave him something to think about during his homeward walk. What connection could Madame Farnienti have with the Rev. Leonard Sterne or Mr. Valentine Gaunt? He grouped them in various attitudes upon his stage, and made them enact various little scenes together; but the mere association of characters so utterly unlike seemed to border upon farce.

These professional studies brought Arnold to the Harrow Road, a very different place from Momus Street, for it was never quiet from morning till night. A stream of cabs and omnibuses and vans was continually rolling along it; hawkers went bawling about with their barrows in the roadway; and all sorts of people jostled one another on the pavement. It was nice and lively, said M. Dubarri, who took the greatest pains to point out its advantages to Arnold. And on a Saturday evening, when the street was always transformed into a regular fair, he declared it reminded him of the Boulevards.

Arnold found him standing on his doorstep, inserting a sweetmeat into the mouth of a tiny girl whose sunny, upturned face looked half-pleased and half-frightened, while a group of other children stood around, waiting their turn, with an excitement they could scarcely control. M. Dubarri's little eyes were twinkling delightedly; and when he had inserted the sweetmeat and closed the wee mouth with his finger, he laughed heartily, and the children began to jump; it was such fun.

It was a new amusement for the old fellow, who was so like a child himself in many ways, that it would have been strange had he not sympathized with the little ones. It must be accounted an extraordinary thing that there were no children in Momus Street, or, at any rate, none visible. The Harrow Road, on the other hand, simply swarmed with them, so that M. Dubarri was in his element. Many knew him already, and never passed the small, shabby house where he lived without pausing to gaze expectantly at the windows. Edged in between two shops, it stood a few paces back from the pavement; and it was here, out of the way of the traffic, that he and his tiny admirers were now collected.

"Ah, ha! You see I am busy, my friend," he cried to Arnold. And though he was smiling, there was some anxiety in his look and tones, as if he was not quite certain how this undemonstrative young Englishman would take it.

Suddenly he gave the rest of the sweet-meats to the children, and, seizing Arnold by the arm, hurried him down the street. It would be difficult to describe the manœuvres that he executed with a view to throwing some imaginary foe off the scent; but he never neglected them when he caught Arnold outside the house on his return from any of his old haunts. After entering a public-house by one door and leaving by another, he seemed more comfortable, though his mind was not altogether easy until they were both inside their own door, which he banged with a deep sigh of relief.

The sitting-room was very like the one in Momus Street. It was about the same size and quite as dingy. If the horsehair couch and chairs were different from the faded green upholstery of the other house, there were the same busts of Shakespeare and Sheridan, the same French prints on the walls, the same ink-stained table-cover, the same books, even the same black cat—a stray cat that M. Dubarri had taken pity upon.

He sat down in the arm-chair, and Arnold occupied the couch opposite. Nothing was said for a few minutes, for they were not quite as talkative as they used to be—a fact

due as much to the din in the street as to
their lengthy companionship.

"I say," exclaimed Arnold presently, "we
have given Mr. Valentine Gaunt the slip."

"That is good, my friend," said M. Dubarri,
shaking with laughter. "He will be blessing
us, that sly old fox, who creeps as quietly as
pussy there. But I am sly, too, and I have
been one too many for him with my little trick.'

"Then you think he will never find us
again ?"

"Never—never, if—— "

"I have so few friends," croaked Mr.
Valentine Gaunt, standing in the doorway,
"that I couldn't bear the thought of parting
with them."

No servant had announced his approach ;
no footstep had sounded in the hall; there
had been no warning knock. The door had
opened noiselessly, and then they saw him
standing there, his foot hovering, his hat held
in his hand, and a malicious smile on his face
as he dragged out his heavy attempt at play-
fulness.

M. Dubarri's face was the funniest sight in
the world, though the poor old fellow was in
a very dreadful state of mind. He was blinking like an owl at that sinister face in the
doorway. He was so dazed that his politeness, which was with him a kind of instinct,
had entirely deserted him ; he kept his seat,
as if he were glued to it. This was, indeed,
a sorry ending to his little trick.

"My friends," said Mr. Valentine Gaunt,
slowly advancing into the room, "seem
scarcely as delighted to see me as I should
have expected."

Perhaps to get rid of his astonishment,
M. Dubarri jumped up and shook himself,
like a Newfoundland dog just emerged from
the water. Then he said dubiously—

"So you have come, my friend! Well——"
an idea struck him and he brightened up,
"we have been expecting you. We knew
you would come, when you found us out.
Mr. Arnold, I would ask you : do I speak the
truth ? "

"No need to answer that, I hope," replied

Arnold, who had viewed this little scene very calmly.

"Eh bien! You are welcome, Mr. Valentine Gaunt. Our departure was so sudden—sapristi! how it incommoded us! And then you are close, we had not your address to write to you. You see, I am frank. Come. I shake you by the hand. Now seat yourself. and after, we shall talk."

He accordingly conducted his visitor to the arm-chair, and, after a little excited dancing about the room, placed himself on the couch by the side of Arnold.

"So you knew I would come," said Mr. Valentine Gaunt, still smiling, "when I found you out, did you?"

"We were quite sure of it, my friend."

"And you were right. I never would desert M. Dubarri. He will understand how deeply grieved I was at losing sight of him for even a few weeks. I can thoroughly enter into the feelings with which he must have thought of me standing at the door of his deserted house."

"Ah! that must have been a sad disappointment," murmured M. Dubarri. Notwithstanding the realization of a fear that
had been haunting him day and night, his
sense of humour proved too strong for his
gravity ; and in order to hide those twinkling
eyes of his, he jumped up, turned his back on
his visitor, and began to stamp his foot, as if
to recover a key that had strayed through a
hole in his pocket. This done, he sat down
and gazed gravely but dubiously at Mr.
Valentine Gaunt, who said—

"It was indeed. But I was so anxious
lest you should think ill of me that I have
lost no time in calling upon you at your new
address. So we shall now be on the same
intimate terms as ever. May I inquire," he
added, watching closely, "what caused such
a sudden change in your plans ? "

"The landlord ; was he not a brute, a
rascal ? I used to tell you so, you will remember. Well, I could not endure the fellow
longer. He said do this ; I wanted to do
that. What could you expect ? We parted,

and—here we are. I am frank, you see.
And you ?   You are quite well, eh ? ”

“ Quite, thank you.”

“ Ah, that is good.   And how did you find
us out, my friend ? ”

“ Mr. Cressingham is an actor.”

“ Bien.”

“ He is in search of an engagement.”

“ Bien,” more impatiently.

“ And he visits a hair-dresser’s shop in
Parnassus Street.”

“ I feared so,” sighed M. Dubarri, losing
all control of his feelings and looking reproachfully at Arnold.   He was scarcely such
a proficient in the art of deception as he
considered himself to be.   “ You followed
him here ? ”

“ A friend told me where he was, for by
the merest accident I happened to be in London
and close at hand.   When we stopped here ”
—his smile struck M. Dubarri as being intensely disagreeable—“ I guessed it was your
house, and waited till your return.   It was
fortunate that I did.”

" Very," was the dry response.

Not knowing what turn affairs might take, Arnold prudently left the room. He had his father's dislike to anything approaching a scene, for one thing ; and for another, thought he might as well seize the opportunity to send a hasty note to Hebe.

A short silence followed his departure, the two eying one another as if they were making experiments in mesmerism. There was fear in M. Dubarri's face, but it changed to something very like the courage of despair, when he said—

" Mr. Gaunt, I shall serve you no longer. It was for that reason I made my escape from the other house. Sapristi ! it is terrible, frightful, this weight hanging round my neck every minute of the day. I can't bear it, so you must do your worst."

" You mean that you will supply me with no more advance-sheets ? "

" That is so. I bitterly repent that I ever supplied you with one. God knows you would never have had another if you had not forced me with threats of exposure. But that is all over now ; my mind is fixed."

" But——— "

" I say it," roared M. Dubarri, banging his fist upon the table. " I am a rock. If you would move me, I tell you it is impossible."

" Then let us say no more about it," said Mr. Valentine Gaunt, in his friendliest manner.

His words so astonished M. Dubarri that he began to blink again. After a while, he leaped from the couch, insisted upon shaking hands several times, and indulged in the most extravagant expressions of gratitude. He had faced the bogey that had been making his life a burden, and lo ! it had vanished. In his frantic glee, he threw prudence to the winds and sent for a bottle of *vin-ordinaire*, the girl receiving the most minute instructions as to how she should carry the bottle.

As a matter of fact, however, Mr. Valentine Gaunt had no idea of relinquishing his prey so easily. His methodical mind was always a little disturbed by an unexpected emergency ; he required time to think it over before he felt himself able to grapple with it successfully. In the present case there was no need to act with haste; the next examination did not come on for several months; between then and now there would be plenty of time to meet this new departure.

It is not a charitable thing to inquire too closely into the cause of repentance. It may be a revolt from the tyranny of the sin itself; it may be a dread of the penalty; most frequently, perhaps, it is a combination of both. But where any doubt exists, it is better to choose the worthier reason. We will, if you please, do this in M. Dubarri's case.

Briefly stated, the facts are these :—

In one of his thoughtless moments, he had mentioned his ability to procure copies of the French papers set by the Civil Service Examiners. Mr. Valentine Gaunt, who was his confidant, immediately set his wits to work, and at length hit upon a method of improving the golden opportunity. He turned tutor by the aid of forged testimonials, written by himself it is almost needless to say, for

M. Dubarri never could have written them.
Indeed, though his signature was used, they
were not even shown to him, for he was too
impulsive to be altogether trusted. He was
merely told that certain inquiries might be
put to him, and he was requested not to
answer them, without reference to the prime
mover in the affair. Of his own free will, he
obtained only one paper; the rest were ex-
torted by means of threats. Had he boldly
taken the bull by the horns, he could no doubt
have defied Mr. Valentine Gaunt, who dared
not proceed with what would certainly have
involved him in a charge of conspiracy; but
this, either through ignorance of the English
law or want of courage, he had not ventured
to do until to-day.

How M. Dubarri got the French papers
is not very certain. He often spoke about
his friendship with one of the examiners, and
he had unmistakably turned Mr. Valentine
Gaunt's eyes in this direction; but then his
way of saying things merely to add to his
own importance, makes this hypothesis more

than doubtful. It is far more probable that
the real culprit was one of the tippling red-
nosed compositors with whom he was acquainted, for such things have been before
and doubtless will again, notwithstanding
such precautions as the numbering of the
papers, the sealing them in packets, and so
forth. However, the explanation is of small
importance; it is only with the fact itself that
we are concerned.

This eventful day had yet another surprise
in store. While Mr. Valentine Gaunt was
drinking *vin-ordinaire* with a courage born of
a desperate wish to appear friendly, and
M. Dubarri was alternately sipping his wine,
and holding up his glass to the light, nodding
and smiling and talking all the time, the
former produced a paper from his pocket, and
handed it to the latter, who settled his *pince-
nez* upon his little saddle of a nose before
looking at it.

"Sapristi! the reverend diable himself!"
cried M. Dubarri, once more lifted to his feet
by the violence of his feelings. "Where did

you get this"—tapping the paper—" this—this ? "

" Will you tell me what I have often asked you ? "

" Why ? You will not answer, so how can I say ? "

" That is my business."

" Well," said M. Dubarri, shrugging his shoulders, " keep your secret, and I shall keep mine. That will be fair play, I think. Here is your picture. Now, let us say no more about it. Come, my friend, I shake you by the hand."

They accordingly shook hands for about the hundredth time.

Mr. Valentine Gaunt left soon afterwards, promising—in response to an invitation that was almost frigid for M. Dubarri, who stood bowing on the doorstep—to call again the very next time he was in town. He had not gone very far when he was joined by Arnold, and the two walked together in the direction of the railway station.

As it was about six o'clock in the evening,

the Harrow Road was in a great state of bustle, due chiefly to those who were returning from their offices in the City. The people overflowed both pavements ; the omnibuses were crammed inside and out ; and innumerable children were hunting one another between the legs of the pedestrians and the wheels of the vehicles. Perambulators were going past in droves, and here and there a loud-voiced butcher stood in his doorway, calling attention to his meat.

Amid this confusion, neither Arnold nor Mr. Valentine Gaunt was likely to have noticed a slight round-shouldered figure— dressed in a blue frock-coat, with the Ribbon of the Legion of Honour in the button-hole, and very baggy light trousers—gliding along a short distance behind. It was a comical notion that M. Dubarri should now be hunting Mr. Valentine Gaunt, whom he had previously suspected of being solely engaged in hunting him. The artful way in which this singular old fellow availed himself of cover, dodging from door to door or lamp-post to lamp-post, showed that he was turning his recent experiences to good account, though he was occasionally rather hampered by some of the young friends to whom he was in the habit of giving sweetmeats.

Suddenly he made a dart for a chemist's shop, for Mr. Valentine Gaunt had stopped in front of a tobacconist's window, and was looking round suspiciously.

"Think over my words, Arnold," he said, holding out his hand. "Don't be discouraged by your apparent failure, and lay to heart the opinion of a friend, that matrimony is the surest road to success. It is a powerful and constant stimulus to exertion; it weans you out of yourself; it makes you do and dare what you would otherwise shrink from. The married man has the madman's strength because——"

"They are much alike," suggested Arnold, raising those unfathomable eyes of his to his companion's frowning face.

"Not at all. But there, I have no more time to spare. I won't forget your letter.

Stick at it, Arnold, and remember if you should be hard up, you know where to come."

It struck him that Arnold showed a very unpleasant degree of irresolution, and as he hurried along the crowded street, he decided that the time had come for taking his next step.

Meanwhile, M. Dubarri, emerging from the chemist's door, slipped across the road to avoid Arnold, and continued his pursuit. Still practising the same crafty tactics, he followed Mr. Valentine Gaunt to the station, at the entrance to which he stood for a few moments, looking in with an uncommonly sly expression, and his finger laid against his nose. But at length, he stole through the booking-office, and gained the platform.

CHAPTER VII.

FALLEN AMONG THIEVES.

PUDDLETON was a charming spot in the month of June, when the sunlight lay deep upon the corn-lands, aglow with scarlet poppies, and the meadows where the cattle clustered under the scanty shade of the poplars. The delightful lanes along which the wagons with their smock-frocked carters moved so dreamily, seemed to have buried themselves deeper in the rolling tide of greenery and colour; and after plunging through some cutting in the sandy soil where the martins had their nests behind a screen of honeysuckle, they vanished altogether. There was at most times a green rivulet of trees and undergrowth running along the base of Camelback and its brother hills, but it broadened at the approach of summer; it poured into little bays here, and surged around promontories there, and so crept up the sunny slopes as if it would reach the blue sky itself.

There was a pleasant drowsiness in the scene. Whether the eye turned to the country smiling back upon a smiling sky, or to the rustic street of red-brick cottages nearly hidden beneath trailing vines or purple bunches of wisteria, and standing in tiny gardens where sunflowers glowed among cabbage-roses and sweet-williams, the prospect was peace. The very Splashwater babbled more softly as it glided under the old bridge; there was a lullaby in its summer song that harmonized with the notes of the cuckoo in the Rectory garden. Only the swallows darting from beneath the eaves seemed to be on the alert, but there was in their smooth flight an absence of effort that rather added to the general effect than otherwise.

Here, at any rate, one might fancy a weary wanderer saying, " I shall find rest."

And now the human element appears upon the scene, and lo! a Babel—a confusion of tongues and many heart-burnings. Putting aside mere noise, of which there was plenty, proceeding from the horns on Silverspoon's coach, the multitude of fox-terriers, and the pupils' band, we pass at once to matters of more importance.

First. of all, there was the Doctor, the autocrat of this little village, a favourite with almost everybody, a wealthy man, and generally reputed prosperous. Yet the haggard look was growing more frequent in his face; it could not be laid aside as readily as it once was; it was leaving its marks in deeper wrinkles, greyer hair, and a slight— very slight—bowing of that wiry figure. The burden was not heavier than it had been for months past; it was, indeed, precisely the same burden; but hope was giving way to despair, and suspense was becoming intolerable—the suspense of waiting for and wondering what would have to be faced next.

Then there was Leonard Sterne, bravely carrying his friends' burdens as well as his own, doing his utmost to help them, yet never knowing whether the next step might not cast him and his wife adrift upon the world.

Then there was Nellie, with her trouble— a very terrible one for the poor girl to have to bear; and Philip with his. He was so bright and hopeful that he might have been the best off of all; and yet to many another, his case would certainly have appeared desperate.

Then there was Hebe, driven almost to distraction by Arnold's unaccountable silence; and Mr. Pike with his fears on her account, and his grievances against the Doctor.

Then there were the pupils, growing daily more unruly and, as a natural consequence, more discontented; and finally the villagers, alarmed lest the disorder should bring about a collapse of the establishment, and render useless the shops they had improved, and the stock they had bought in order to tempt the pupils.

Here, then, in this pretty, peaceful-looking village, we find a great deal of uneasiness and a great deal of actual misery, not of the kind that is inseparable from existence, but due mainly to the selfishness of one man—Mr. Valentime Gaunt—whose free-and-easy ways made him generally popular, and who played his part with such caution that most laid the blame upon Leonard Sterne. Still, in his determination to get rid of his dangerous rival, he might go too far, and perish in the ruin that he himself had caused. There was just this peril to be avoided, and it was one of the chief reasons why Mr. Valentine Gaunt advanced with such extreme deliberation.

About this time, as if there was not quite enough trouble, a cloud of locusts descended upon Puddleton with the intention of devouring every green thing. It must be confessed that in the whole wide world they could not have found a better site for their operations. Puddleton was full of green things, though they wore big-check suits, and tootled on coach-horns, and strummed on banjos in their baths.

The locusts were money-lenders, who came in the guise of touting tailors, tobacconists, wine-merchants, and so forth. The steady-going Heavisides, who was of luxurious habits, had picked up a specimen somewhere in the neighbourhood of his Militia regiment during the annual training, and had brought it down to Puddleton, the eventual result being to bring his strong-minded mother upon the scene. There were in the bill certain items that she strongly objected to pay, and she carried her objections into court with very fair success. Fancy waistcoats purchased by the dozen were declared not to be necessary for a gentleman's outfit; so they were struck out, together with many other things. But it turned out that only some of the huge number of suits set down to the account of our cylindrical young friend, were to be found in his wardrobe; the rest represented money lent at an enormous rate of interest. This, of course, had to be refunded, though the interest was cancelled. Finally, the touting tailor was told very plainly what the judge thought of him.

Unfortunately, Mrs. Heavisides' lawsuit proved hurtful in one way. It brought Puddleton into notoriety, and a swarm came where there had hitherto been only a single specimen. They kept dropping into the street, like insects after a thunderstorm. Of course it fell to the lot of Leonard Sterne to clear them away; and a very disagreeable task it was, though here he had all the villagers on his side.

The most troublesome of the pests was a certain Vampiretti: an uncommonly obliging fellow by his own showing, but a most insatiable bloodsucker, according to others. He was seldom observed about the village in person, and yet he was acquainted with the names of the pupils and kept showering upon them circulars setting forth his singular generosity. He was so pertinacious that, after dodging the inhospitable bootjack, and flying before the deftly-hurled poker, he would appear again next morning, smiling and bowing at the door, while he offered you any amount of money merely for the honour of your patronage, with, perhaps, a *post obit* thrown in.

This creature—it seems a libel upon the race to call him a man—contrived to get very many of the pupils into his net, and among the number was Plantagenet. The matter became talked about in the village, and was eventually told by Gammon to Leonard Sterne, who thereupon laid it before the Doctor in his study.

" If we don't take care," said the Doctor, twitching his glasses from his nose and leaning back in his chair, " between the two stools of usury and general disorder, we shall come to the ground. I'll tell you what it is, Sterne ; we must make an example of some- body." He spoke with a certain satisfaction, and it almost seemed as if there ought to be a smile slyly lurking in the depth of those keen small eyes. " The discipline of the place demands an instant sacrifice; the higher, the better. I have made up my mind that Plantagenet must go. Won't that astonish them?"

Sterne looked greatly astonished himself.

"Yes," he said; "but I should call Plantagenet about the best of the lot."

"All the better—all the better. It will strike all the more terror into them. It will keep them quiet for a time, and then out comes another victim to the wolves."

"Is it quite fair?"

"But surely you agree with me that discipline must be maintained?" said the Doctor, ranging himself with comical dexterity on the side of order, and inviting the staunch disciplinarian to come and join him.

"There is Heavisides, for example."

"Mr. Sterne," said the Doctor, solemnly, "Heavisides will be here for another ten years."

The wish is proverbially said to be the father to the thought; but in course of time the son shakes off the paternal yoke and leads a sturdy independent existence. The matter-of-fact way in which the Doctor spoke, showed that he had brought himself to believe in the stability of his establishment, and that this belief had not been shattered by recent events, even though the idea of lasting fame might have to be abandoned. If he could have faced the possibility of seeing his ambition destroyed during his lifetime, he might have defied Mr. Valentine Gaunt; but the man of method had gauged his strength as well as his weakness.

The Doctor followed up his announcement to Sterne by its prompt execution. Higgins was at once despatched to pack up Plantagenet's things, and when this young gentleman returned from a drive on Silverspoon's coach, he was surprised to find all his portmanteaus on the top of a fly, waiting to convey him to Stilbury. In the utmost indignation, he rushed up to the Rectory to expostulate with the Doctor, or at least to learn what offence he had committed. The Doctor was asleep and could not be disturbed;

such was the message brought out by that
sphinx, Higgins, whose gravity, however,
scarcely concealed a suspicion of a smile.
Plantagenet next went to the Hut, but
Sterne could merely reiterate the Doctor's
orders. In the end, he left in high dudgeon
and amid the sympathetic cheers of a crowd
of friends.

There can be no doubt that this incident
created a profound impression; the pupils
being as quiet as mice for the next few days.
But it very soon turned out that the Doctor
had been indulging, as usual, in a little
sleight-of-hand, yet with such a masterly air
of sincerity as to have deceived even Leonard
Sterne. Why, he could no more have dismissed the son of a duke than he could have
flown.

Before Plantagenet reached home, his father
received a letter from the Doctor, detailing
the transactions with Vampiretti and stating
that as Lord Ernest had been growing a
little wild of late, it was considered necessary
to check the tendency at once : " in which,"

added the Doctor, "I feel sure your Grace will agree with me, so I have packed him off home in order to give him a fright. A week's rest will do him no harm, and then we shall be ready to receive him again." Hence it was that a week later Plantagenet returned to Puddleton, and was greeted with quite an ovation, Heavisides even going out to meet him, along the Stilbury Road, smiling and strumming upon his banjo.

Sterne, who, with all his opportunities, had scarcely fathomed a current of humour underlying the Doctor's character, felt bound to put in a very serious protest. "Such vacillation," he said, "was utterly subversive of discipline."

"Bless the man, he's never satisfied," exclaimed the Doctor. "Why, you yourself declared Plantagenet to be the best of the lot, and now that I have him back, you are still grumbling."

"Not at the fact itself," objected Sterne, as gravely as ever, "but at the principle involved. If you had not given people to understand that you were sending Plantagenet away altogether, I should see no harm in your taking him back."

"But did I give people to understand that?"

"Well, not by words——"

All the lightness had vanished from the Doctor's manner, and he sighed wearily.

"The effect upon the pupils has been good," he said. "You can see that for yourself. I have tried the same thing before, and it has never failed me. And, Sterne, my friend"—the wistful look in his careworn face was full of pathos—"these little ways of mine give me almost the only pleasure that I have left. If *you* are going to object to them now, I shall be beset on every side."

These were sad words, indeed. They lighted up with a sudden glare the depths into which this unfortunate foolish old man had fallen. They simply appalled Leonard Sterne, who could scarcely conceive such hopeless misery. He could not understand this delight in overreaching others, and saw only its worst qualities; the very idea of being driven to it alone for distraction made him shudder. He was nearly imploring the Doctor to tell him the nature of the mysterious power possessed by Mr. Valentine Gaunt, but want of perfect confidence came between them again, as it had often done before.

Sterne uttered no further remonstrance. He spoke in his kindliest and most cheery manner, and then sadly went homewards, trying hard to unravel the tangled threads.

In his study he found one of his favourite pupils, a nice little fellow called Sparrow Hawk. Though quite a boy, he had not escaped the contagion of extravagance, and alarmed at the dismissal of Plantagenet—of whose return only an hour before he had not yet heard—he had at length prevailed upon himself to make a clean breast of it. The Doctor found a pretence of knowledge that he did not actually possess, to be a very serviceable weapon at times; and this, no doubt, had proved effective in the present case. At any rate, Sparrow Hawk seemed to think that his secret had escaped from his keeping. To cut his long story short, he had fallen into the clutches of that fiend, Vampiretti. He was very miserable over it and very penitent, and not a little afraid of his father's anger. His conduct, though reprehensible, did not amount to a heinous sin, in Sterne's opinion; so he did his utmost to reassure the lad. First of all, he said, he must consult the Doctor; which he accordingly did.

"Start away for Hastings by the next train, Sterne," said the Doctor. "Sir Kestrel Hawk is there now, and if he is the man I take him to be, he will help us to clip the wings of this scoundrel, Vampiretti. Off you go—*tout-de-suite!*" And he banged his fist upon the table.

If the Doctor was fond of promptitude, Sterne liked to show that he was not destitute of that quality. He packed up a small hand-bag, telegraphed to the baronet to announce his intention, hired a fly from the Lark's-Nest, and was soon rattling along the road to

Stilbury. The same evening he arrived at Hastings, or rather St. Leonard's, his destination being one of the large houses on the Marina.

He was very courteously received by Sir Kestrel Hawk, a fierce-looking man with prominent eyes and red hair and moustache. The baronet was proud of his blue blood, and it showed very distinctly in the veins of his forehead. When he heard Sterne's account of what had happened, he was perfectly furious. It was the first time, he declared, a member of his family had ever made a fool of himself, and he was determined it should be the last, if he could help it. As Sir Kestrel's wrath against his foolish young son cooled down, it grew hotter against the rapacious usurer, who, it appeared, had tried to evade the minority clause by means of an agreement that the loan and interest should be regarded as the price of certain worthless cigars that Sparrow had received from him.

"I shan't pay him a penny," said the baronet, "not a penny. Let him sue me, if

he dare! Equity is on my side; and law——
Well, I'm not a prophet. The law and the
prophets always go together. But even if I
should lose the case, I would have the
pleasure of exposing the fellow, and, perhaps,
stopping his rascality."

"Quite so," assented Sterne, who saw that
the Doctor had not mistaken his man.

"And now let us leave an unpleasant
subject," said the baronet. "Of course, Mr.
Sterne, you will sleep here this evening. I
have asked a few friends to dinner."

"I shall be very pleased, Sir Kestrel. In
any case, I could not return to my work till
to-morrow."

And thus it came about that eight o'clock
found Leonard Sterne seated at the baronet's
dinner-table with half a dozen other guests.
The room was large and handsomely furnished.
It contained a great number of foreign
curiosities, chiefly Indian; but better than
all, it looked out upon the sea—a sheeny
gently-heaving sea dotted about with white-
sailed boats, and merging into pink and

crimson clouds, which formed a glorious mountain landscape upon the horizon. The murmur of the waves floating in through the open window, the footmen gliding about with their silver dishes, the soft buzz of conversation, the strangeness of the pretty things around—all tended to throw Sterne into a dreamy mood; from which he was aroused by a remark made by one of his neighbours, an elderly white-headed clergyman who had been introduced as Mr. Knight.

It was a reference to Mrs. Heavisides that had arrested Sterne's attention. In answer to his inquiry, it appeared that during the season she belonged to Mr. Knight's congregation; and, on account of her famous lecture—so he called it—at Exeter Hall, he held her in the highest esteem. He then went on to speak in terms of reprobation of her steady-going son, whom he described as going downhill with a rapidity that scarcely justified his sobriquet. This led Sterne to mention his own connection with Puddleton.

" The name of Copingstone," said Mr.

Knight, " is so un—no, no more wine, thank .
you, Sir Kestrel—so uncommon that I should
think there can be only one family in
existence."

" There is only one, I believe," answered
Sterne.

" The other day, in looking over my
register, I came across the name. It was a
marriage, I think, but I forget the particulars."

" I should greatly like to see it."

" You can see it, with pleasure."

Sterne made an arrangement for the
following day.

Next morning he took leave of the baronet;
and although it was a little out of his way,
strolled along the sea-wall as far as the baths,
where the band was playing and a well-
dressed crowd collected. It was a pretty
scene, with the feathery clouds floating in the
blue sky overhead, and the sunlight glancing
upon the water—an almost limitless expanse
of opalescent colours, were it not for Beachy
Head frowning out of the haze in the far east.

Sterne turned from the bright faces around

to the merry children playing on the beach; everybody seemed happy but himself, and he felt a strange depression of spirits. Afterwards he told himself that it was due to a presentiment of coming evil, but there can be no doubt that the real cause was his being sadly out of harmony with his surroundings, for nothing makes a man feel his trouble more keenly than this does.

With a sigh Sterne hurried away.

He found Mr. Knight waiting for him at the church door, and together they entered the vestry—a dismal little cell pervaded by one of those close bottled-up smells that are difficult to classify. It may have proceeded from the clerical gear—some of which looked much the worse for wear—hanging from a nail in the door, or from a couple of musty umbrellas in the corner.

"You don't look very well, Mr. Sterne," said the kindly, white-headed old clergyman.

"Perhaps your Hastings air is rather stronger than that of Puddleton," suggested Sterne, euphoniously alluding to the smell in question.

" Ah, I dare say." And he dragged the heavy book from its oaken chest and laid it upon the table.

He began to turn over the pages, while Sterne stood watching with an anxiety that he could scarcely conceal and could not account for. When, at length, the entry was found and pointed out to him, he stooped down to read it.

" Good gracious, sir, sit down in that chair," exclaimed Mr. Knight. " Would you like a glass of water ? "

" No, thank you," replied Sterne, whose face had turned deadly white. " It is a merely passing spasm. I'll take a copy of this, if I may."

" Certainly ; but are you sure I can't do anything for you ? "

" Quite, thank you."

Sterne sat down in the chair. Then he brought out his pocket-book and copied into it the words that had produced such a painful effect upon him.

CHAPTER VIII.

A DIFFICULT PROBLEM.

The passion-flowers peeping from the snow-storm of clematis that had nearly buried the Rectory, were a pretty sight; but not so pretty as Nellie standing in the porch, with the sunlight falling in a golden flood upon her dainty figure, and her hand raised to shade her blue eyes. She was looking after her father, who was riding down the gravel sweep between the laurels, the coachman following to close the gate.

Mounted on his showy cob, the Doctor was a sufficiently picturesque object in his high sloping hat and Wellington boots. He sat so firm and square in the saddle that none could have guessed his age, until he turned to wave his hand to Nellie, when his grey beard told a tale that a smiling face could not belie.

It was an unusual thing for him to go out for his afternoon ride without Nellie. But she said that she was not very well, and, indeed, she had been looking pale for some weeks. At one time he would scarcely have liked to leave her alone, for fear of the ardent young lover who had boldly declared his intention of seeing her as often as possible; but latterly a restraint had arisen between the two, and it pleased as well as puzzled the Doctor. He was pleased because Philip kept away from the Rectory, and Nellie showed no anxiety to meet him; and puzzled at certain inconsistencies in their behaviour when chance happened to bring them together. Nellie had made up her mind to avoid all society until the mystery concerning herself was cleared up; and, as for Philip, he had consented to take Leonard Sterne's advice and wait patiently for a while. But this, of course, the Doctor did not know, and was not likely to know, for it was not his way to make any inquiries direct. So, while he wondered a good deal, he merely kept his eyes open and told Higgins to do the same.

When her father had ridden out of sight, Nellie returned to the drawing-room and her book. She was not left very long in peace, however. A quarter of an hour later the door opened, and Mr. Valentine Gaunt was announced.

He entered with a rush. Yes, it was a very decided rush ; only every detail, even to the way in which he carried his hat and stick and the glove that he had just taken off his right hand, had the appearance of careful study. He seldom wore gloves, except when paying a ceremonious visit to the Rectory ; and on these occasions he assumed a sprightly demeanour, all the more remarkable for its contrast with his cautious movements in general.

There was one other peculiarity about him that must be noticed. His hair had gradually been growing darker. It had once been unmistakably grey, mutton-chop whiskers and all; but while it was still scanty, still carefully brushed across the bare patches, the colour was now a uniform brown. It is easier to record the fact than to explain it. Some people grow younger in one way, and some in another; but the approach of this second childhood had affected Mr. Valentine Gaunt in other things, besides his hair.

He greeted Nellie with almost boyish effusion, and yet with a tinge of affected bashfulness which was really very funny. Her coldness chilled him a little, but not much. He had evidently prepared his part up to a certain point, beyond which he would have to trust to his own resources.

Sitting on the couch opposite Nellie, who knew perfectly well what was coming, Mr. Valentine Gaunt took something from his pocket and held it so that she could see it.

"Your photograph!" he said, and his attitude and tones were most theatrical. "Your photograph! I have carried it about with me for weeks and weeks. It has been my constant companion."

"May I ask where you got it, Mr. Gaunt?" interrupted Nellie, rather alarmed and greatly astonished.

" Well, I have come prepared to tell you that," replied Mr. Valentine Gaunt with an air of frankness that M. Dubarri could not have surpassed. "I feel sure, when you know the circumstances, you will pardon what I did. I—in fact, I took it out of your album."

" I should call that stealing."

" Have I been the only thief? There are other things that can be stolen besides photographs. There are hearts. Oh, Nellie—— "

The abominable fellow was actually on his knees. He did it just as if he had been practising before a mirror.

" Excuse me, Mr. Gaunt," again interrupted Nellie, rising with a dignity that would have been laughable under less painful circumstances, "I am Miss Copingstone to all but my intimate friends."

" But—— "

Mr. Valentine Gaunt was obliged to scramble to his feet, for Nellie was deliberately walking out of the room. Standing within the space enclosed by the three couches, he looked after her retreating figure with mortification and anger, his cheek-bones glowing like live coals. Clearly he had made a mistake.

"Stop!" he said hoarsely, his hand fluttering in the air.

Nellie, who had gained the door, turned and confronted him. Her pale face was slightly flushed, and her lips were quivering, but otherwise she showed no sign of agitation.

"I thought it more respectful to you," he went on, "to come to you first. In future I shall be compelled to approach you through your father."

It was a comical speech, sounding just as if he was afraid of her.

"Whose money you care for, and not me," indignantly added Nellie, who understood the threat. "Do you think that by persecuting him you are likely to advance

yourself in my estimation? Oh, I am not
quite blind."

"The Rev. Leonard Sterne," announced
Higgins, throwing open the door.

The situation was so obvious that Sterne
hesitated to advance; but Nellie, glad enough
of the interruption, welcomed him eagerly.
He had only just returned from St. Leonard's,
and, having met the Doctor riding along the
Stilbury Road, had come to the Rectory to
see her alone. In this hope he was not
disappointed.

After sitting for some time in gloomy
silence, Mr. Valentine Gaunt at length
departed, with less sprightliness than when
he entered. He had rather expected a check,
but not such a serious one as he had received.
In fact, he now perceived that he had underestimated Nellie's keenness of penetration—
that the particularly pleasant manner he had
always assumed for her especial benefit had
been altogether wasted. However, he congratulated himself upon having two strings
to his bow. Doubtless the Doctor would

prove more amenable to reason; if not, another application of the screw would do all that was required. On the whole, Mr. Valentine Gaunt saw no cause to despair of reaching the highest point of the ladder up which he had been methodically working his way, and wounded vanity was only an additional incentive to success. He had already learnt what could be done by a determined man, even when starting under very dubious conditions; and he felt confident that by pursuing the same method, always keeping one end in view and mastering each detail before passing on to the next, he must reach his goal eventually.

Sterne's object in calling at the Rectory was to ascertain the exact wording of the entry in the family Bible. Nellie had no difficulty in satisfying him on this point, for it was deeply imprinted upon her memory. He wrote down what she dictated to him, and, without telling her his motive, returned to his study, where he proceeded to give the matter his most earnest thought. He lighted his old briarwood pipe as an aid to reflection, and, resting his forehead in his hands, began to pore over his pocket-book, which lay open upon the writing-table before him.

Here is what perplexed and troubled him:

The entry in the register at Mr. Knight's church certified the marriage of the Rev. Cyprian Claude Copingstone, bachelor, to Mary Burnett, spinster, just two years after Arnold's birth. Sterne had also succeeded in finding the registration of Nellie's birth—but not Arnold's—eighteen months after her parents' marriage. This latter date he knew to be correct: at least, so far as the day of the month was concerned, for he had often given her presents on her birthday. The one entry, therefore, tended to corroborate the other.

On the other hand, according to the family Bible, the Rev. Claude Cyprian Copingstone, bachelor, was married in a church near Birmingham to Mary Morgan, spinster, at a date four years previous to that mentioned in the other entry; and while Arnold's birth was stated to have occurred two years after the marriage, Nellie's name was not given at all.

How were these extraordinary contradictions to be reconciled? Had the Doctor been married twice? If so, what object had he in concealing the first marriage? how came he to be described each time as a bachelor? why did he allow Arnold and Nellie to be regarded as brother and sister? and why was not the case fully and frankly stated in the family Bible? But perhaps the second marriage was merely a repetition of the first, rendered necessary by some strange mistake in the names. Were it not for the fact that there is often no small amount of mental confusion at a wedding, the inversion of the Doctor's Christian names would really have a very strong appearance of fraud. Was this the meaning of "the old Adam" and the Doctor's aversion to anything likely to bring him into notice, except among the particular set from whom his pupils were recruited? Finally, did the secret of Mr. Valentine Gaunt's power lie somewhere within this net-

work of mysterious circumstances, improbable
as it had appeared at first?

Such were only a few of the disquieting
questions that passed through Leonard
Sterne's mind, until he grew quite dazed
with following them. There was no sequence
among them, not a single bond of union;
everything contradicted everything else.
Out of the inextricable entanglement, he
could draw but one clear idea: that he must
make a desperate appeal to the Doctor to
confide in him. Even if his attempt should
be as unsuccessful as experience had taught
him to expect, he would at least clear his
conscience of any reproach of underhand
dealings.

This determination will show that his faith
was as firm as ever, otherwise he would never
have run the risk of having it shattered
completely. No doubt, he still told himself,
when the matter came to be explained, it
would turn out to have been merely some
youthful prank, the consequences of which
had been purposely magnified by Mr. Valen-

tine Gaunt until at last they seemed to the
Doctor to threaten his life-long ambition. It
was a charitable theory, yet scarcely a rational
one; the theory of a true friend, as Sterne
was, almost above all else. He made no
attempt to fit these last discoveries in with it;
he knew he could not do so at present, and
contented himself with the explanation that
he had not yet sufficient material to work
upon. It was a foolish thing, he felt, to try
to make bricks without straw; even if he
succeeded, the house built with them would
be a very fragile erection.

So Sterne rose from the writing-table and
went downstairs to the drawing-room window
in order to watch for the Doctor, who shortly
afterwards came jogging along the street,
nodding pleasantly upon all, and sometimes
stopping to chat with one of his poorer
parishioners. As he rode by, some of the
pupils were lolling upon the bridge, and their
faces instantly brightened. Gammon was
bowing and beaming from his doorway, and
opposite stood a number of smiling school

children dropping funny little curtsies, which were duly acknowledged. If Sterne had wavered before, such a sight as this could not have failed to reassure him. The Doctor had a way of diffusing sunlight wherever he went, and it was not until he had gone that a doubt ever arose as to whether it was genuine or some artificial substitute.

Sterne met him outside the Hut and walked alongside as far as the Rectory gate, where the Doctor dismounted. The coachman, who was always able to calculate his master's return almost to the minute, took charge of the cob, and the two clergymen entered the Rectory.

In the study Sterne narrated what had come to his knowledge, omitting all reference to Nellie's share in the matter.

The Doctor looked a little startled at first, but his expression soon settled down to one of anxious thought. His habitual promptitude was due not to want of caution, but to the fact of his being a quick thinker; and here was a new and complicated problem that could not be solved in a moment. He was evidently undergoing a severe mental struggle. While he hesitated, he kept glancing at Sterne as if he was calculating the probable effect of each sentence that presented itself. At length he took up a pen and began to fidget with it; a bad sign, very soon verified.

Had the Doctor been less afraid of Sterne's rigid morality, which admitted forgiveness as a Christian principle but was apt to ignore it in point of fact, he would probably have seized the opportunity of sharing his troubles with a confidant; but as it was, he merely ran away from the difficulty.

"You have tumbled upon a mare's nest, Sterne," he said hurriedly. "I could set you right if I chose, but I don't see any object in doing so—none at all. And now what did Sir Kestrel say?"

"Well," said Sterne gravely, "if you won't let your friend help you, he must see what he can do by himself."

The Doctor looked up uneasily.

"Do you doubt me?" he asked.

" Certainly not. But I fear that you doubt me."

" Not at all, my friend, not at all. Pray, don't misunderstand my silence. The more precautions, the fewer accidents. I like to erect a bulwark against circumstance, which often makes tools of men, however strong they may be."

Sterne naturally saw in this casuistry an admission of what it was meant to deny. He saw in it, also, an unconscious revelation of character. The Doctor's general suspiciousness, then, proceeded from the fact that he considered mankind to be not inherently bad, but inherently weak; and it was a fair inference that he reasoned—unwittingly perhaps—from a knowledge of himself. Sterne felt inclined to resent the imputation in his own case, but it glanced off without doing any damage, for he knew that his chief fault lay in the very opposite direction. At the same time, he was pleased at having a slightly better light thrown upon what he regarded as the most objectionable quality in the

Doctor; and this enabled him to look at recent events with a courage that, to others, might scarcely seem justified by circumstances.

"I don't agree with you, Dr. Copingstone," he declared firmly. "It is due to myself to say that; but I am certainly not so foolish as to argue against what I know to be a deeply rooted conviction. I must repeat, however, that, if I possibly can, I intend to help you against yourself."

"Do your worst, Sterne," laughed the Doctor, knowing that unless something very unexpected should turn up, Sterne could do absolutely nothing. Moreover, it gave him a certain sense of security to feel that henceforth he was to have an active ally whose operations could not be hurtful and might be beneficial. He was not very clear about the nature of this possible benefit; but when a man is desperate, he seldom pauses for any logical hair-splitting.

Sterne hesitated on his way to the door. For one moment, he thought of urging Nellie's distress as a last argument, but here

again the old obstacle cropped up. The
father must not be provoked into telling the
daughter an untruth for the sake of setting
her mind to rest. Apart from the evil itself,
if she were ever to find it out, her faith and
love would be severely shaken, when she
discovered him to be different from what she
had fondly supposed. Whatever else happened, this must be avoided. As Sterne had
foreseen all along, he had to act alone. It
was almost a relief to feel that his action
would be quite unhampered. The first thing
to be done was to verify the entries in the
family Bible. They might be incorrect; at
any rate, the same importance could not be
attached to them as to a formal registration.

He was again sitting in his own study,
when it dawned upon him for the first time
that there was something more in the matter
than he had imagined. The supposed motive
seemed insufficient to account for the Doctor's
obstinate reticence. If it was merely a fear
for the stability of his establishment, why
should he not confide in him who was also

interested in that stability? Surely there was something else—something that he wished for its own sake to hide from the world. Could he for any reason be ashamed of his first wife, and anxious to keep her name from his children? Sterne pursued this new vein for some time, leaving out of account, however, the effect of his own character upon the Doctor.

His meditations were interrupted by the entrance of Philip Strathclyde. His bright young face was much flushed, and he was evidently in a state of great excitement.

"Two gigantic discoveries," he announced.

"Have you found out what is Mr. Jostler's small suggestion?" laughed Sterne.

"No. But I have found out that Mr. Gaunt was an actor before he came here, and that his real name is Valentine."

"Indeed!" observed Sterne, gravely.

"Yes; and now we see why he knew so much about Shakespeare, and so little about anything else, and why everything he does is just like acting."

"Where did you get your information, Philip?"

"You remember that French beggar, the man who startled the Doctor. Well, when Mildred was outside the Lodge gates this afternoon, he slouched up and spoke to her in rather a threatening way. Fortunately I happened to be close by, so I just collared him. He called himself Jacques somebody, and said he wanted to see a Mr. Valentine, and then it all came out."

"I don't see," said Sterne, still restrained by the old anxiety not to be prejudiced by jealousy, "that it is of any importance. There is no reason why a man should not take another name in addition to his own; indeed, he is often obliged by will to do so. And if Mr. Gaunt was an actor at one time, that is certainly nothing against his character."

Sterne was quite free from the old-fashioned ideas on this subject. As we have already seen, he was fond of theatre-going himself.

Philip looked sadly disappointed.

" I thought the Doctor would have kicked him out," he said.

" He is not in the habit of applying his Wellington boots to any such purpose," said Sterne, laughing.

" At any rate, it is certain now that this is Mr. Gaunt's first tutorship ; and if so—— "

He stopped and looked doubtfully at Sterne.

" You must get that idea out of your head, Philip," said Sterne, warmly.

Philip, he knew, was alluding to the possibility of the Doctor's having been mixed up in that affair of the French papers. It was a charge that he would not entertain for a single moment. But it brought forcibly to his mind the strange absence of foreign tutors from Puddleton, and especially the difficulty about the testimonials. He had taken neither of these things into his calculations, and yet they seemed to call for some explanation.

However, the only chance of success in his troublesome task lay in his following one thread at a time. On the next day, the pupils were to play a cricket-match against

Stilbury; and as no work would be done, Sterne determined to seize the opportunity of going to Birmingham. He could then inspect the register and return by the last train.

CHAPTER IX.

DRIFTING.

" I LAUGH," said M. Dubarri, suiting the action to the word. "Sapristi! how I laugh!"

Holding the lappet of his coat with one hand, and flourishing the other in the air, he was standing on the hearthrug, shaking with laughter, which even the noise in the Harrow Road could not deaden. He had just returned from his hunt after Mr. Valentine Gaunt, and had found Arnold lolling on the couch.

"I think I am not a fool," proceeded M. Dubarri, growing calmer; " but he is as sly as a weasel, that rascal Mr. Valentine Gaunt. You did not know I was after you, eh?"

"I have been so accustomed to see you in

the van that I should never have dreamed of
looking for you in the rear."

" He is a cunning rascal. I fear that fellow.
But what is bad for me, is bad for him, too.
We are in the same boat, you know, my
friend."

" Throw him overboard," drawled Arnold,
" and pray that the sea won't throw him up
again."

_" That is my wish, but he escapes me
always. I watched the train like a lynx. I
saw him get in, and I said to myself, ' Now
I shall have your address, without doubt, my
friend.' So I waited until the last moment
and then crept slyly up, smiling at my clever-
ness, and looked in at the window—*ma foi*,
he is gone. The compartment is empty.
How did he do it ? "

He looked as pleased as if he himself had
done something wonderful. Herein, he differed from the Doctor, who could see no joke
in anything that victimized himself; whereas
M. Dubarri could, if only he could understand it, and had some one to laugh with him.

"Perhaps he was under the seat," suggested Arnold.

"*Mais non*," cried M. Dubarri, with a self-satisfied smile. "I say to myself: 'You shall not baffle me there, my friend.' And so I open the door and search; but it is useless."

The idea of M. Dubarri searching for the portly form of Mr. Valentine Gaunt under the seat struck Arnold as so funny that he began to laugh, and the good-natured old fellow at once chimed in.

"I saw him enter, I do assure you," he said; "the whole time I never took my eyes away from the door; and when I went to look, he was gone. Imagine my astonishment! He comes without sound; he goes without being seen. I begin to fear that man."

"He must have slipped out through the other door by means of a railway-key."

"Ah!" In his excitement he knocked over a small vase that stood upon the mantel-shelf. It fell to the floor and was broken.

"*N'importe*," he exclaimed, shrugging his shoulders and then brushing the pieces aside with his foot. For tidiness was not one of M. Dubarri's virtues.

A slip of paper had tumbled out of the broken vase. It was the same slip that had thrown him into a violent state of agitation on a previous occasion, though Arnold did not recognize it until he had picked it up and accidentally read it. The paper was yellow and crumpled, and the ink faded. It contained merely the signature, " C. C. Coping-stone."

Arnold perceived the handwriting to be his father's, and a faint glance of curiosity came into his eyes, but died out again so quickly as to escape detection. Leaning back in his chair, he held out the paper and said carelessly—

" Is this yours? An uncommon name, I should think. It would suit a pillar of the church."

" The reverend diable himself," muttered M. Dubarri, hurriedly thrusting the paper in

his pocket. " I hunt for him everywhere—
up and down—up and down ; but in vain. I
should like to have him upon toast, as your
English proverb says."

" Upon toast ? "

" Yes, poulticed with cayenne-pepper."

"Rather warm treatment," observed Arnold,
slowly raising his eyes to look at this ferocious
old fellow. " What has he done ? "

" Let me be frank," said M. Dubarri, as
if it were a task of some difficulty. " He
has done "—he hesitated, and his little eyes
began to blink—"nothing, my friend, nothing
at all."

Knowing M. Dubarri to be an able con-
cocter of fiction, Arnold naturally ascribed
his latest effort to that class. Nothing was
more easily obtained than an autograph, provided that it was not attached to a promise to
pay ; and upon this possession, M. Dubarri
had evidently constructed some ingenious
theory ; in any case, it was not a thing to
bother one's head about.

There was much of the good-tempered

mastiff about Arnold in character, as well as
in build. When he first heard the uncom-
plimentary allusion to his father, he felt
inclined to get up and shake the too loquacious
little Frenchman; but on second thoughts
decided that it was not worth while, especially
when no insult was intended.

Nothing of any importance occurred until
the following Wednesday afternoon, when
Mr. Valentine Gaunt again appeared, creep-
ing into the house in the same stealthy way
as before. He was very fond of paying these
flying visits to town. On a half-holiday he
often left Puddleton at the conclusion of work
and returned by the last train at night, or
sometimes by the newspaper train in the
morning. In either case, his absence did not
interfere with his tutorial duties, and the
Hivites seemed to be very happy without
him. Latterly, however, at the Doctor's
particular request, he had always asked
Mr. Jostler to act as his substitute when he
intended to be absent all night.

His attitude towards M. Dubarri was most

friendly. He spoke as if he wished the past to be forgotten ; and the rollicking way in which, after unfastening the straps of his travelling-rug, he brought out a bottle of champagne, was proof of his intention to make a fresh start. He made no reference to any peculiarity connected with his departure on the occasion of his last visit. If there had been anything of the sort, he preferred to ignore it.

Whenever he could do so unobserved, M. Dubarri blinked at him wonderingly. Though he had a profound belief in his knowledge of human nature, he felt that here was a case a little out of the common. He seemed to have awakened out of a horrible nightmare to find that his supposed enemy was, after all, his friend. What had caused this transformation ? He was wise enough to put sentiment out of the question. After reflection he concluded that his recent behaviour had made his fellow-conspirator afraid of treachery.

There was some truth in M. Dubarri's conclusion, but Mr. Valentine Gaunt had not misjudged him to this extent. He was still waiting. It was only when he found it necessary to clear any obstacles out of his path, that he became disagreeable—intensely disagreeable to the obstacles; and there was no need to hurry at present. Perhaps he might attain his end by pleasant means; if so, all the better; if not, he was fully prepared to strike when the time came. Meanwhile, his visit was not to M. Dubarri at all, though it would have the excellent effect of showing him that he was under observation; it was really to Arnold, a terribly sluggish fellow, who required continual prodding to keep him moving.

Mr. Valentine Gaunt took the earliest opportunity of making his purpose clear by means of a wink; and after bidding M. Dubarri a very cordial farewell, sauntered quietly down the Harrow Road, where he was presently joined by Arnold. They walked slowly on towards the station. The street not being so crowded as usual, it was easy to see that they were not being followed this time, though Mr. Valentine Gaunt threw many suspicious glances over his shoulder.

He wished to urge, he said, the benefit of an immediate marriage. He spoke out of the purest friendship; indeed, what other motive could he have? If money was the objection, he would gladly place his purse at Arnold's disposal, and only regretted that the sum he could spare should be so trifling. There was Hebe spoiling her pretty face by weeping and pining; the poor girl was beginning to look desperately ill; surely Arnold ought to have some regard for her feelings! He didn't say this reproachfully; not at all; only, being a friend to both, he was able to look at both sides of the question.

Arnold, however, was not so easily moved. Knowing nothing about the course of events in Puddleton, he could not conceive why he was being urged to take a step that, considering his present circumstances, would be little short of suicidal. Moreover, he had latterly begun to doubt the sincerity of Mr. Valentine Gaunt's friendship. It seemed overdone ; the mainspring to which he sedulously directed attention was scarcely strong enough to move all the works. He reminded Arnold of a ventriloquist, guiding the eyes of his audience to the particular spot from which he wished them to think the sound proceeded.

That Mr. Valentine Gaunt was irritated at his defeat was clear enough, for he banged a red-hot explosive at the head of a mechanic who happened to run against him; but when he turned to Arnold he was sweetness itself.

" I suppose money is the obstacle," he said. " Well, you know the old adage, Arnold : ' It is just as easy to feed two mouths as one,' while, on the other hand, you must remember that two heads are better than one. Look what a careless, good-natured fellow you are ! What you waste, a clever, thrifty wife like Miss Hebe would save. You are a lucky fellow, Arnold, you are, indeed; but come, I'll say you deserve your luck."

" I haven't got it yet," said Arnold.

"Still, there it is, ready for you. Of course, in advising you to marry, I am going against my own interests, for I am incurring the risk of offending your father."

"Say no more, Mr. Gaunt," interrupted Arnold. "I couldn't allow you to do such a thing. You have given me the best of all reasons why I should act on my own responsibility."

Mr. Valentine Gaunt looked greatly annoyed. Though he had proceeded with his usual caution, he had, in some strange way, contrived to overstep the bounds of prudence. The worst of it was, he could see no chance of retrieving his position. He protested most strenuously that Arnold had mistaken his meaning; and brought up a battalion of arguments to prove his case, but without the smallest effect. It was really most vexatious. If he had not been careful to work out another method, he would have been in an awkward fix. It was not quite so safe, for which reason he would rather have avoided it; but he would take every precaution, and, practically, had no alternative. Before he made his final move, it was absolutely necessary to prevent the possibility of an alliance between the Doctor and Arnold. Doubtless many would think that this had been accomplished already, but it was just because he differed from the many that he had succeeded so far—he liked to " make assurance doubly sure."

Mr. Valentine Gaunt soon mastered any outward expression of disappointment. When he saw that nothing was to be gained by continuing the subject, he dropped it, and assumed the *rôle* of the jovial companion. He induced Arnold to accompany him to the station in order to have a parting drink at the refreshment bar ; and when he left, carried with him a letter to Hebe, which he had no intention of delivering. This was the beginning of his new departure.

Arnold had no suspicion of treachery ; merely the slight distrust already mentioned. He waited on the platform, talking to Mr. Valentine Gaunt until the guard's whistle sounded ; and then, with a wave of the hand, started on his way alone.

The weather had been muggy all day, and when he got outside the station he found it had begun to rain. " Only a shower, sir," a policeman said ; but instead of waiting, Arnold pulled up his coat collar and strode through the heavy drizzle. In the Harrow Road he met M. Dubarri, politely escorting an old lady, who no doubt found his umbrella useful, in spite of a big hole in the cover and its two broken ribs. Though he seldom went anywhere without the melancholy umbrella in a silk case, which modestly concealed its deficiencies, he never used it except upon such occasions as the present, for he delighted in rendering these little services.

After bowing the old lady into the post-office, he dived into a confectioner's, and, emerging with a small parcel of sweetmeats for his young friends, hooked his arm into Arnold's ; and so the two walked together.

M. Dubarri took up his favourite position on the hearthrug, with his back to the grate.

He preferred it, because it gave him a commanding view of the room.

"My friend," he said, unbuttoning his frock-coat so as to show his waistcoat, "observe!"

He was holding the coat wide open.

"I can see nothing," said Arnold in some perplexity.

M. Dubarri smiled and nodded.

"Now observe!"

And he slapped a handful of silver and some gold upon the table.

"Money!" said Arnold.

M. Dubarri smiled and nodded again. When he had returned the coins to his pocket, he sat down with the air of a conjuror who has performed a successful trick.

"I had no idea the funds had sunk so low as that," said Arnold, to whom it now occurred that M. Dubarri's gold chain had disappeared. "Why didn't you tell me? Here, you must take my watch."

But M. Dubarri waved it back. "*Mais non —mais non*," he cried. "Keep your watch,

my friend. We may have to eat it by-and-
by, but I have a few little things that can go
to the uncle, as you call him, first. What is
the good of two watches in the same house?
They are a nuisance, for they never agree.
But one—that is another thing entirely."

"You are a kind old fellow, M. Dubarri,"
said Arnold, "but you must not prevent me
from contributing to the joint purse. Is that
all the money we have?"

"There are my books."

"This is really horrible."

"My pupils," said M. Dubarri, stretching
out his hands, "where are they? I wait for
them and they do not come; I hunt for them
and find not one; when I go to interview a
parent, he looks at me with his nose in the
air. 'Bah!' he says to himself, 'you grey-
bearded old fellow, you must be a fool or a
knave, or you would not be wanting work at
a shilling an hour.' So nobody will have
anything to do with me. And you, my
friend, those stupid managers will not engage
you. I have no patience with the fellows.

But "—his face brightened wonderfully— "cheer up, my friend, cheer up. We shall make our fortunes yet, I do assure you. Let us be jolly. I shall go and buy two bloaters for our supper."

Still smiling, he seized his hat and dashed out; but when he found himself alone in the hall, he stopped to wipe away the moisture that had been gathering in his eyes. He soon mastered his weakness, however; worked it off by vigorously brushing his frock-coat, now carefully buttoned to hide the absence of the gold chain that he had been so fond of displaying. Then he sallied out with a cheerful face and a grand air, which, at the sight of a little girl whom he knew, he instantly dropped in order to fumble in his pockets for his parcel of sweetmeats.

Though M. Dubarri had, until now, concealed the real state of affairs from his young friend, they had gradually been drifting into very troubled waters. Before long, starvation would be staring them in the face. The one, of course, could fall back upon his father,

and might be driven to do so, however much
he might dislike it after his short struggle
for independence; but the other had no such
resource. For him, the position seemed well-
nigh desperate. He had already dismissed
the pale-faced servant girl, and cut down the
household expenses to the bare necessaries of
existence; he had quite given up his bottle
of *vin ordinaire*, and seldom smoked a
cigarette, saying that it no longer agreed
with him; and though he contrived to have
dinners that made a very fair show, there
was rarely little else. M. Dubarri appeared
to possess the remarkable power of adapting
his appetite to his means; and now, while he
took care that Arnold was never stinted, he
scarcely ate anything himself. Still, considering that the day could not be very far
distant when he would not have a morsel of
bread to put into his mouth, it was strange
how the old fellow managed to keep up his
spirits as he did.

In the dark days that followed, he was
sorely tempted to make a few pounds in the

old way. He had once decided that not for
a prince's ransom would he again pass under
the yoke, but now that he compared the
sufferings which were past with those which
were as yet in anticipation, he almost felt
inclined to reconsider his decision. He
thought of the galling journeys—over which
he pretended to laugh—to the pawnshop,
with now a parcel of books, and now an
article of furniture, and, lastly, a bundle of
clothes; he thought of the time when the
pawnshop would be no longer available—when
scanty dinners had given place to no dinners
at all, and he, a feeble old man, whom
nobody would employ, trudged aimlessly
about the streets, eagerly scanning the gutters
for a fallen copper, or peering wistfully
through a confectioner's window at the things
for the want of which he was starving; and
then his mind went on to a time when even
this was too much for his wasted strength—
when nothing remained but to crouch in his
cheerless room, praying for a merciful release
at the hands of Death. Truly, an awful

prospect. That he fought against his temptation at all, shows that his lesson had been a
severe one.

It was fortunate that Mr. Valentine Gaunt
did not know what a powerful ally he had in
this dread of starvation; when he came to
know, who could say how the struggle would
go? M. Dubarri guarded his secret with
jealous care; he was always scrupulously
dressed, always cheerful, and the very pink
of politeness. Though liable to brief intervals
of depression, he never really lost heart,
which was due in no small measure to a
sanguine expectation that he or Arnold might
tumble into a fortune at any moment. He
had not the remotest idea where it was to
come from, but like Mr. Micawber, was
always expecting "something to turn up,"
the something being invariably an almost
fabulous amount.

Towards the end of June, a number of
suspicious-looking men got into the habit of
calling at the house. They all had some
thing to say for themselves: one mentioned

taxes, another rent, another water, another
gas, and so through all the dismal catalogue.
M. Dubarri received them with great ceremony, just as if they were honoured guests,
but it made one's heart ache to see his smile
and all the other painful efforts to hide his
distress. He told them frankly that at
present he had scarcely a penny in the world,
but that he expected to have a large fortune
in a short time.

One evening he was in the act of bowing
two of them out—they sometimes hunted in
couples—when the postman stopped at the
door and handed him a letter for Arnold.
It was the first letter that had come for this
strange young fellow, who seemed to have
no past and no family, and whose loneliness
had deeply touched his impressionable companion as well as excited his curiosity.

M. Dubarri grasped the letter with trembling
eagerness. Here was the long-looked-for
fortune come at last. No child could have
been more excited than he was. He never
gave a thought to the fact that the sup-

posed good luck was not for him, but for
his friend, their interests having been so
closely allied in the past that he was unable
to dissociate them in the future. When he
had perched his *pince-nez* on his little turned-
up nose, he inspected the envelope, which
bore the London postmark. The address was
in a woman's handwriting. Not from a
theatrical manager, then. He rushed into
the sitting-room, and gave the letter to
Arnold without a word; he was too agitated
to speak. Then he stood opposite, watching
with intense anxiety.

The letter was from Hebe Pike. It stated,
very briefly, that she was staying with a
married schoolfellow, who lived in Bayswater,
that she had run away from Puddleton in
order to marry Arnold at once, and that she
hoped to see him that evening.

Here was a dreadful dilemma. Marry
when he was on the brink of starvation!
And yet how was marriage to be delayed
for even a few days when Hebe had com-
promised herself with all her friends and

relations ? What could have induced her to act in this rash way ? She was usually so thoughtful.

"Well, my friend?" said M. Dubarri very sadly, for he had guessed that it was not the fortune after all.

"There is something here that I can't understand," replied Arnold, rising to his feet. "I must go and see about it. When I return, I may be able to explain."

CHAPTER X.

A STRANGE MISSION.

IT was a glorious June morning; Camelback rising from its lacework festoons into a deep blue sky, and the Splashwater gliding down the green slopes with a merry song, which the breeze carried softly past the creeper-clad houses to the sunlit fields beyond. The air was warm and summer-scented; it was full of the indistinct murmur of insect life, so different from the death-like silence of a winter day; and from the copse of fir trees that formed a pretty background to the church, with the ivy clinging around its ancient belfry, came the cooing of a wood-pigeon.

In the rustic street the pupils were

gathered in groups, while a few of the villagers in cricketing attire were standing a short distance away. There was young Joseph Haply who had played for the county; and Mr. Smirke, a famous slogger in county matches, his knack of putting every ball to square leg being especially admired; and George Whittle, brother of the carrier, who had acquired a great reputation for long-stopping the fastest bowling with his un-padded shins; and several others, all glancing dubiously at the "young gentlemen"—un-certain whether to join them at once on equal terms, or whether to wait and grow chummy on the field, or perhaps at "the cold collation" in the tent. Mr. Valentine Gaunt —also in flannels, though he was not going to play—was hovering about, chatting plea-santly to everybody; and there also, stroking his long beard, was Mr. Jostler, creating dreadful panics by bearing down upon each group in turn with the evident intention of offering a small suggestion.

When many of the groups had melted

away, an empty fly drove along the street
and stopped at the Hut. It was watched
with curious interest, volleys of questions
were fired at the head of the driver, and
Gammon and the worthy postmaster darted
simultaneously to their respective doors. It
required but a very little thing to raise a
great commotion in Puddleton. Heavisides,
smilingly strumming upon his banjo, sauntered up in order to inquire who was going
away, and was answered, " Mr. Sterne, sir."
He resolved to wait, and, after clambering
up the stone pillar of the gate, sat there
strumming.

Heavisides was far too good-natured and
easy-going to have imbibed any of the violent
prejudices against the austere outspoken
clergyman; prejudices that would never be
allowed to die so long as Mr. Valentine
Gaunt was to the fore. If they had led to
no open breach of discipline of late, it was
simply because he was engaged in binding
the final cord around the Doctor, before
getting rid—as he firmly meant to do—of a

man whose interests were opposed to his, and whose force of character would be a constant source of danger.

Still, notwithstanding the comparative quietude, Sterne was growing more unpopular. It was seldom enough that he acted for his own benefit, and yet everything he did, even his raid upon the money-lenders, was turned against him. Vampiretti, whom Sir Kestrel Hawk absolutely declined to pay, was making it uncomfortable for his other clients; and the Doctor having with his usual adroitness slipped his own head out of the noose and substituted Sterne's, the latter found himself very awkwardly situated. In fact, he had become a sort of ogre to the pupils, and it was quite a fashion to say nasty things about him.

There were some, however—perhaps many, if the truth were known—who secretly admired him for having the courage of his convictions; and among the number was Heavisides, whose feelings ran a good deal deeper than his thoughts. He sometimes took it into his head to speak out, but as it was not supposed that he could say anything worth listening to, he was only laughed at for his pains. Nevertheless he was not to be deterred from showing a shy sympathy for Sterne, and it was with the intention of playing to him a nigger melody that he had taken his seat upon the stone pillar in front of the Hut.

Sitting up there, the good-hearted fellow was a remarkable object, his broad face beaming with the mere pleasure of existence upon this sunny day, and his short cylindrical figure clad in a velveteen jacket, fancy waistcoat, and corduroy trousers, the whole surmounted by a huge Panama straw hat. Several of his friends stopped to chaff him, but he merely smiled and went on strumming.

He struck up " Poor dog Tray "—it was the only tune he could get anywhere near— when at length Sterne, putting on the tasselled hat, came running down the steps. A glance from the pupils standing with their backs towards him to the quaint musician was enough to explain the situation; he felt touched at the lad's kindness.

"Good morning, Mr. Sterne," said Heavisides cheerily. "Going away?"

"Yes, I'm off to Birmingham. That's a pretty tune you are playing."

"I like it; and I think I'm a little better at the banjo than I am at Latin." On the previous day, he had translated "Arma virumque cano" as "A man with an arm and a dog." He gave a sort of nervous chuckle at the reminiscence.

Sterne, also, could not resist a smile. "You like the banjo," he said kindly, "and you don't like Latin; that makes all the difference. But if you'll only give your heart to your work, I think we'll manage to pull you through your examination yet."

"Thank you, Mr. Sterne. That's more than Mr. Gaunt ever said."

He scrambled down from his perch and, as Sterne took his seat in the open fly, grasped his hand.

And now the others, who had been watching this little scene from a distance, came trickling up. They looked very sheepish at first, but a few kind words set them at their ease, and they were soon talking together like a number of old friends. Indeed, it was quite like old times again. When the fly drove away, they all joined with Heavisides, who was radiant with delight, in wishing the clergyman a pleasant journey.

The incident made a deeper impression upon Sterne than he would have cared to admit. He had neither the Doctor's love of popularity for its own sake, nor Mr. Valentine Gaunt's for the sake of its power; but like most of us who respect ourselves, he fully appreciated the respect of others. Their approval made his path far smoother; it transformed a wearisome task into a real pleasure. So it was with a lighter heart than he had had for many a long day, that Sterne started on his mission. And what a strange mission it was! he reflected. To find out something in the life of a friend who, by a few words, could save him all the

trouble! To help that friend, it almost
seemed, against his own wish! But was not
he doing unto others only what he would
have them do unto him? Possibly the strong
vein of enthusiasm in his nature was apt to
lead him into extravagances; the pupils
thought so when he tilted against the many
abuses in vogue; the parishioners thought so
when, in the teeth of a powerful opposition,
led by Mr. Pike, the people's churchwarden,
he reformed the service by the introduction
of a surpliced choir and good music; but
he differed from them both, and held that he
was right, as firmly now as he had ever
done. And surely it was no extravagance to
help his friend, if not for his sake, at least
for his daughter's! There could be no doubt
that the Doctor was every day finding his
burden heavier to bear; yet, unless something were done, its weight would soon be
increased tenfold, for that little scene in the
Rectory drawing-room showed plainly Mr.
Valentine Gaunt's intentions. He was the
cause of all the mischief—yes, Sterne felt he

could say it dispassionately now—and if he were only out of the place, a better order of things would again prevail; the pupils, as he had just seen, being easily led, and really good fellows at heart.

While the fly was passing the cricket-field, Sterne stood up to watch what was going on. It was a large square meadow, fairly level in the centre, but very rough near the sod-fences, which were flanked by lofty poplars, framing here a red-brick cottage, embedded in an orchard, and there a picture of golden corn and scarlet poppies.

Some gipsies had erected an "Aunt Sally" in one corner of the field, and a number of the pupils and villagers were shying at cocoanuts; several others were having a preliminary practice in out-of-the-way spots; and near the gate was a large tent, in front of which some smock-frocked old fellows were sitting on benches, watching the game with a very solemn and critical air, sometimes shaking their heads sadly, as if modern cricket were a sorry sight, and it were indeed a melancholy thing for them to be obliged to witness it. At intervals they were so overcome that they had to take refuge in great mugs of beer, which stood in the grass at their feet. Even when Mr. Smirke, who happened to be in, ran out and slogged the Stilbury slow bowler out of the field—when everybody else, amid a profound hush, was watching the ball in its flight over the poplars, these dismal old fellows were still shaking their heads; and one of them pointed to a distant field as if it were quite an ordinary occurrence in his day to put a ball there. Instead of joining in the applause when Mr. Smirke came out to refresh himself with a glass of beer after his supreme effort, they again fell back upon their mugs.

And so they passed out of Sterne's sight. He was sorry to part with them, for he was an enthusiastic cricketer and would have been playing to-day had it not been for his self-imposed task.

He was on the point of sitting down, when, chancing to look on the other side of the

road, he caught a glimpse of a tall thin
figure, in a high sloping hat, that he knew
well. It was the Doctor, standing with bent
head behind the fence. Nellie was with him,
and her head also was bent down, though it
could not have been seen from the road if
she had stood on tiptoe. The Doctor always
made a practice of watching the cricket for
an hour or so; and, with this intention, had
evidently followed the path across the fields,
and was about to pass through the wicket-
gate close to which he was hiding. But
why? He looked ill and white and worn,
Sterne thought, and yet there was a sly
twinkle in his eyes. He was not watching
the fly now, but perhaps had been doing so
and did not expect its occupant to turn
round. He seemed amused rather than
alarmed. There was a smile, too, on Nellie's
pretty face, and she had laid the tip of her
finger on her rosy lips as if to enforce silence.

Sterne glanced behind, and the mystery
was explained. Mr. Jostler, if you please,
prowling about in search of somebody to

deliver a speech to. As bad luck would have it, he took it into his head to look over the gate; and the last that Sterne saw of him was trying to button-hole the Doctor. To the astonishment of his driver, he burst out laughing. If we had only these little troubles to contend against, he thought, what a delightful world it would be!

In less than an hour Sterne was being whirled away towards the Black Country. It was not a very long journey that lay before him, and he had arranged to travel by a fast train, with only one change. He expected to reach his destination early in the afternoon. But before that time arrived a fog seemed to rise out of the earth and gradually to increase in density. Heavy clouds hung over the horizon, and presently the sun became merely a red globe suspended in the dingiest of skies. Then arose a forest of tall chimneys, filling the air with smoke, and all the ground around was black as night. The very cottages that clustered around the factories, were black; and nature seemed to have dwindled down to a monotony of rubbish-heaps interspersed with pools of inky water. But after a while the sun began to look more respectable again; and the train, after stopping at several insignificant stations, rushed into Birmingham, a town of many miserable streets and many magnificent buildings.

In Stephenson Place, a short street running down to the station, there was a perfect mob of iron-masters and metal-brokers, haggling over "pigs" as if they were pork-merchants. They were gathered so thickly around the Exchange that Sterne had great difficulty in pushing his way through them. He had at first intended to adopt the cheaper plan of walking to his destination; but when he reached the cab-stand at the top of the street, changed his mind and entered a hansom, drawn by a very wooden-legged horse. There was a fashionably dressed crowd in New Street, carriages were rattling to and fro, and the number of ladies bent on shopping this fine afternoon was really astonishing. They all passed before Leonard Sterne as in a dream, and when he arrived in a prettily wooded country, with handsome houses peeping from bowers of trees, he was still more surprised, for he had expected to see little beyond grimy workshops and smoke.

It was at a picturesque old church, with a picturesque old Rectory close by, that the hansom eventually stopped. After telling the driver to wait, Sterne alighted and entered the churchyard in order to explore. At the same moment the Rector, with a bunch of heavy keys in his hand, appeared in the porch. He was a short, stout, good-humoured-looking old man, who carried his head on one side like a sparrow. He introduced himself as Mr. Nash, and he and Sterne were soon on a very friendly footing.

"Oh yes," said Mr. Nash, in answer to Sterne's inquiry, "I remember Mr. Coping-stone very well indeed, a tall, thin man, with a shrewd face and a peculiar laugh. He was curate here when I was presented to the living, but he resigned shortly afterwards."

"Why was that?"

" Well, to tell the truth, I don't think he
cared much about church work. And then
he got married, took that house over yonder"
—he walked to the corner of the church, and,
laying his head still more on one side, pointed
to a house about two hundred yards down
the road—"and confined his attention to
teaching two or three pupils. He left rather
suddenly, and nobody knew why."

" And what family had he then, Mr.
Nash ? "

" Oh! only a wife and a son about four
years old. I baptized the child myself, and
can show you the entry, if you like, Mr.
Sterne. It will enable us to approximate to
his age, at any rate."

This affable old gentleman, who evidently
supposed the Doctor to be no longer alive,
seemed very pleased to act the showman.
He trotted into the porch, the keys jangling
by his side, and trotted up the aisle, pausing
now and again to point out the beauties of
his church, and finally trotted into the vestry;
a very similar cell to that other in Hastings,

but without the bottled-up smell of stale umbrellas.

Sterne followed in a dazed, wondering way. The farther he wandered into this mystery, the more bewildering it became. It was now clear that when the Doctor left Birmingham, he went almost direct to Puddleton, for there was a difference of only a couple of months between the two dates. Yet he had left with only a single child, Arnold, and arrived with two children, Arnold and Nellie, the latter being then a year old.

Sterne was shown the registration not only of Arnold's baptism, but also of the marriage of the Rev. Claude Cyprian Copingstone to Mary Morgan, and both corresponded with the entries in the family Bible. It was really a very shocking entanglement. If any reliance could be placed upon documentary evidence, the Doctor had married a second wife while his first was still alive, and had contrived to keep two families going at the same time. This was quite incredible. Then, had he, owing to some informality in the

names, married the same wife a second time?
But if so, where did Nellie come from? On
the other hand, unless there was something
wrong, how was Mr. Valentine Gaunt's power
to be explained?

"Would you tell me, Mr. Nash," asked
Sterne, desperately, "what Miss Morgan—I
mean Mrs. Copingstone, was like?"

Mr. Nash complied with alacrity. His
description satisfied Sterne that she was the
Mrs. Copingstone whom he had known.

"Do you know anything about her relations?" he inquired.

"No, nothing. But I rather fancy that
she was an orphan. She came here as a
governess to a family who some years ago
migrated to Australia; but she was with
them only a short time. Mr. Copingstone
had a very prompt way of doing things,"
said Mr. Nash, laughing. "He came, saw,
and conquered Miss Morgan. The courtship
lasted about a week; then the engagement
was announced, and the house taken; and a
fortnight later they were married."

It was just like the Doctor. Sterne was obliged to smile, strange as the whole affair was.

"I married them myself," pursued the old clergyman, rubbing his hands and smiling as if he were recalling a particularly pleasant incident, "and a quieter, more business-like wedding I have never officiated at. Let me see, he must have been ordained then about —ah," and he cocked his head to peer up at a shelf above the table, "I have an old clerical directory there : that will tell us."

Sterne was placed in a dilemma, though this was nothing new. He scarcely liked to say that the Doctor's name was not in the directory, and yet it seemed almost deceitful to remain silent. While he was hesitating, however, Mr. Nash had mounted a chair, and brought down the book. He opened it and, turning to the proper page, laid his finger upon it.

"Here, you see—— "

"Indeed !" interrupted Sterne, in great confusion. And hastily bending over the directory, he beheld the name of the Rev. Claude Cyprian Copingstone. He could scarcely believe his own eyes, it was such an astonishing thing. Was the Doctor really hiding in Puddleton? It seemed very like it. If so, for some absurdly exaggerated reason, of course, but what could it be?

"Have you any other old directories?" asked Sterne.

"Yes, I have one in my library: for the year after Mr. Copingstone left here, I think. Come along and see it. And, dear me, what a forgetful man I am. You must be hungry after your journey. My wife will give you something to eat."

And so chatting, the old clergyman trotted off again, turning his head round occasionally to peep at his companion. He stopped to lock the church door, and, when Sterne had beckoned to the cabman to follow them to the Rectory, they proceeded there together.

Mr. Nash was a very lively old gentleman. He had ushered his visitor into the library, and found the directory before Sterne had

had time to look about him. For a moment
or two he hesitated to open the book ; and
when he did so, was scarcely surprised to
find that the name of the Rev. Claude Cyprian
Copingstone was omitted.

CHAPTER XI.

HEBE'S FLIGHT.

HEBE'S flight, which occurred a few days after Sterne's return from Birmingham, created a great commotion in Puddleton. The village gossips, not caring to plead ignorance, looked marvellously knowing about it: all except Mr. Valentine Gaunt, who showed as much surprise when he was told the news for the hundredth time as when it was first announced to him. "It really was a most unaccountable thing," he declared. Whereupon Gammon, Whittle, and the rest proceeded to enlighten him. "Hebe," they said, putting forward their conjectures as facts, "had run away to marry Arnold at Oxford, because she was ill-treated at home."

Mr. Valentine Gaunt replied that he could not believe it.

It was about seven o'clock in the evening when the rumour first began to get abroad. Who started it, nobody seemed to know, but it soon spread like wildfire. When the sun settled down in the glowing west and the shadows of the poplars stretched far over the silent fields, the village street was filled with groups, all eagerly discussing this marvel. There were the pupils with their fox-terriers; smock-frocked old fellows with hoes over their shoulders; young men just returned from the cricket-field; women with babies in their arms; and among them all moved a line of sleek cows, driven by a rosy-cheeked little girl.

Mr. Pike's house was, of course, the chief centre of interest. It was a pretty two-storied building with lattice windows and a profusion of Virginian creeper. Shrinking modestly from the public gaze, it stood in an old-fashioned garden, and there was a large chestnut tree planted before the door. Gam-

mon, Whittle, and many others were standing not very far away, watching it curiously.
At the same time, more than one wore an
air of great importance, as becoming the
possessors of special information.

Though he had attached no particular significance to the fact until now, it appeared
that Whittle had during the last week con-
veyed three boxes for Hebe to Stilbury, to be
left at the station till called for. It was also
ascertained from Mr. Smirke that she had not
hired a vehicle from him; and as Gammon
had observed her starting to walk towards
Stilbury about noon, since which time no one
had seen her, it was clear that she had gone
on foot. This settled the manner of her
departure, and also the fact that she had
carefully arranged it beforehand.

" That, sirs, I know for certain," announced
Joseph Haply, determined not to be beaten
in the production of news. He paused and
dealt out a lofty smile to everybody alike,
before he added : " And I'll tell you why."

" Ah ! " said Gammon, " I thought the

postmaster had got something on his mind, for he's been going about all the afternoon like a pig that's ripe for the knife."

The postmaster acknowledged the compliment with a grunt of satisfaction. He was very red in the face and very round in the body, and he lurched about like an old Dutch brig in a smart breeze.

" Well," he said, the roll in his voice hinting at an intention to make the most of his news, " it was yesterday morning about half-past eleven, or maybe a few minutes after; anyway, I was in the shop at the time, getting a penny bottle of ink for Mrs. James Hodge, though I rather think it was meant for James himself, and my daughter had just gone out to see after the despatch of the mail, when who should come in but Miss Hebe herself in a blue dress—you'll remember the one she sometimes wears, Mr. Gammon ? "

" Ay, ay ! but what are you driving at, postmaster ? " The butcher spoke rather impatiently, for he felt that such rigid accuracy was out of place.

" Driving at ? Ain't I telling you as fast as I can ? When I had finished off Mrs. James Hodge, I crossed the shop to attend to Miss Hebe—she was standing at the post-office counter—and what do you think, sir, she said to me ? "

" Oh, get along, postmaster, do ! " exclaimed Gammon. " How do we know ? "

" You might guess, anyway. She said she wanted to draw all her money—a tidy sum, mind you—out of the savings bank."

He stopped in annoyance, for he had suddenly lost the attention of his audience. They were gazing at the pretty two-storied house that sheltered itself behind the chestnut tree.

The door was open, and framed among the Virginian creeper stood Mr. Pike, with his inquiring nose, big moustache, and painfully stiff collar. He turned the whole of his short plump body to look up the street, and then turned it to look down the street, and seeing the number of people about, he hesitated. But somebody, probably his wife, spoke to

him from the house, and he strutted out
more pompously than ever.

It was a dreadful thing that he had just
returned to hear—Hebe disgraced in the eyes
of all who knew her! No doubt he would
have welcomed her marriage with Arnold;
and perhaps, suspecting their attachment, he
was to blame for not having insisted upon its
being either recognized or else broken off
entirely. But this disaster was surely a
severe penalty to pay for want of judgment.
He felt only sorrow and pity for his daughter;
but he was very bitter indeed against Arnold,
who, he was convinced, had induced her to
commit this rash act. If it had not been too
late to catch a train from Stilbury, he would
have started for Oxford at once, tired as he
was with a long drive. He meant to go next
morning, and meanwhile to have it out with
the Doctor.

Arnold was generally supposed to be still
at the University. Philip knew that he was
not there, and was greatly exercised in his
mind as to how he should act. So also did

Mr. Valentine Gaunt, who intended to turn his knowledge to good account. But all the others were utterly in the dark, so successful had been the deception practised by the foolish old Doctor, who continued playing off the same miserable devices in the hope of finding his son. The approach of the Long Vacation had thrown him into great difficulties. New excuses had to be invented; he had to plunge deeper into the mire, while Mr. Valentine Gaunt stood and looked on with a detestable smile on his detestable face; and now, as if his troubles had not been bad enough, here was Hebe running away.

The news gave the Doctor a terrible shock; he could no longer doubt that she and Arnold had been in correspondence, though since intercepting the one letter he had felt safe in that respect. It was equally certain that the two were bent upon getting married. He had not the smallest idea of Arnold's occupation, tuition being the only thing that occurred to him, but it gave him some comfort to think that his son, badly as he had behaved, was not embarrassed by financial difficulties, otherwise he would never dream of marriage.

When the Doctor could look at the matter more calmly, he was not so sure that he had viewed Hebe's flight in the proper light. There is usually something to track a woman by when she travels: a railway porter who has toiled under her luggage, a cabman whom she has ground down to the uttermost farthing, another to whom she has cheerfully paid double fare, and often a paper parcel or bandbox dropped here and there along the route.

Was not it likely, then, that Hebe might give a clue to Arnold's address? The firm of private detectives who had all along been engaged in the search, with the result of periodically finding the wrong person, would now have something to work upon. If the young couple were discovered before the marriage, it might be nipped in the bud, notwithstanding the fact that both were over age, Hebe only just. After all, the prospect might be worse.

But the Doctor forgot Mr. Pike, who was pretty certain to follow in his daughter's track. If he were to find the young couple, no end of unpleasant complications might ensue.

Mr. Pike strutted up the street as if he were moved by springs, and the way in which he twisted his body round to exchange " Good evening " with first one acquaintance and then another only added to the effect. He never had been so pompous before ; and yet the poor old man was merely trying to check his excessive nervousness. It was no easy matter to appear composed before all those curious watchers, especially when he knew what they had been talking about. It would be difficult to say whether the pitying looks of the women or the half-amused looks of the men were the harder to bear.

Of the many marks of sympathy shown to him, the one that affected him most was a glimpse of Mr. Valentine Gaunt gliding swiftly into Whittle's shop at his approach. It was, he felt, the act of a thorough gentleman, quick to penetrate the feelings of others and equally quick to humour them. All that he wanted was to be left alone with his trouble—to go his way unseen and unspoken to ; and this nobody seemed to realize except Mr. Valentine Gaunt. There was a strange mist in Mr. Pike's eyes as he reached the Rectory gate. He paused, ostensibly for the purpose of polishing his bald head, but really to brighten his vision. But when he remembered the object of his visit, his face hardened again; he put his handkerchief away, strutted up to the door, and knocked.

By means of an ingenious arrangement of mirrors, not easily detected by those ignorant of the secret, the Doctor, while sitting at the writing-table in his study, could see any one entering the Rectory. He was, therefore, quite prepared when the lawyer was announced by Higgins. Having a strong objection to being taken unawares, his impromptus were generally the result of careful forethought. He had no difficulty in guessing the object of this visit; and as he was as ready to defend Arnold and attack

Hebe as Mr. Pike was to attack Arnold and defend Hebe, some lively skirmishing ensued.

If Mr. Pike was polite, the Doctor was urbanity itself. He insisted upon his visitor's taking the armchair, which he placed facing the light, while he himself took a less comfortable seat with his back to the window. Neither seemed inclined to approach the subject of their thoughts, but at length Mr. Pike ventured on the ice.

" You may have heard, Dr. Copingstone," he said, sitting bolt upright, " that my daughter has disappeared ? "

" Indeed—indeed! A rumour to that effect has reached me, but I could scarcely credit it." Though he certainly had a fellow-feeling for the bereaved father, he felt that he must look to his own interests. " I sincerely trust you have not come to confirm it."

Mr. Pike shook his head.

" I am so sorry," said the Doctor, " so very sorry, that I scarcely know what to say by way of consolation."

"It is reported in the village that she has gone away to be married to your son."

The Doctor looked astounded.

"Scandal," he said, "an absurd scandal. I'm sure you'll agree with that, Mr. Pike."

"Then what action do you propose to take in the matter?"

"None at all. I can afford to despise it."

"But I can't, Dr. Copingstone," returned Mr. Pike, warmly, "for the reputation of my daughter is at stake. She has been wheedled into this disgraceful act by your son——"

"Hold there, Mr. Pike!" said the Doctor sternly, with an imperious gesture. "Before you go any further, give me the proof of that statement."

Mr. Pike turned very red in the face. In the capacity of a father he had committed a most unprofessional blunder.

"There was," he stammered, "a strong attachment between them——"

"Hold there again, Mr. Pike! Have they been in correspondence during the last nine months?"

" Not to my knowledge."

" Quite so ; otherwise I am sure you would have interfered. And what is more, if any letters had passed between them, the fact would have been known to everybody in the village."

" They might have been directed to a third person. At any rate, there is only one way to settle the matter. I am going to Oxford to-morrow. Your son is there now, I suppose ?"

" No, Mr. Pike, he is not. The Long Vacation has commenced."

" Then," said Mr. Pike, courteously, for he was pleased at his escape from an untenable position, " will you kindly oblige me with his address ?"

He might just as well set about fishing for the sea-serpent with mackerel tackle. The Doctor, placed in a difficulty from which nothing but virtuous indignation upon some side issue could save him, rose to his feet. And then, laying his hand upon the back of his chair, this tall, thin, grey-haired clergyman looked down upon the pompous little bald-headed lawyer, who was suffering from a very similar heart-ache, and said, haughtily—

"No, sir, I'll do nothing of the sort. If you can't trust your daughter, I hope I can trust my son."

The storm was tropical in its suddenness and severity, but the heat was artificial. It was almost as surprising as a tornado in a hot-house would be.

When the first shock of astonishment had passed away, Mr. Pike also stood up—very carefully, because of his stiff collar. The hand that held his hat was trembling, as if he had been stricken with the ague; the other was clasping the border of his coat. Angry as he looked, he was determined to control his feelings, one mistake being quite enough.

"A word before I go, Dr. Copingstone," he said hoarsely.

The Doctor walked to the bell and rang it.

"If," continued Mr. Pike, "my daughter comes to any harm at your son's hands, you shall rue it to the last day of your life."

The door opened and Higgins stood there, bowing his white head, and looking the very picture of polished ease, yet watchful withal; a strange contrast to the lawyer and the clergyman.

"Door, Higgins," said the Doctor.

Mr. Pike gave him one angry look, and then strutted out into the dusky twilight, which was lending a new beauty to the landscape. It was some comfort to see that fewer people were standing about, though every door and window was wide open. On his way down the street, he passed irresolutely in front of the Hut. Should he make an appeal to Sterne? But no, the whole lot of them were leagued together; there was no more chance of getting the truth out of one than out of another. He must depend solely upon his own resources. First of all, he would go to London—that huge bundle of hay where every missing needle is supposed to be hidden—and search high and low until he had found Hebe; and if she and Arnold should be together, he would then have a safe position from which to attack the Doctor.

It was a sad evening for the lawyer and his wife. They were angry with the Doctor and his family, angry with his tutors, angry even with his pupils whose shouts they occasionally heard outside; but when they thought of their absent daughter, they were melted to tears. If the dangers that they dreaded were only imaginary, they were none the less terrible. In answer to a telegram sent to the station-master at Stilbury, they learned that Hebe had claimed her boxes there and taken a ticket for London. More than this they did not know. But both felt certain that she had gone to Arnold, wherever he was.

Meanwhile the Doctor, left in possession of the field, behaved very unlike a conqueror. He drew the armchair up to the writing-table, sank wearily into it, and rested his head in his hands. His sigh was full of heaviness, and the expression of his face was like that of a hunted animal. He was beginning to doubt the efficacy of his own cunning—to wonder whether, after all, a straightforward course was not the best in the long run. Continually dogged by Mr. Valentine Gaunt, he knew not which way to turn; every step he took only plunged him into worse difficulties. Yet how could he retreat now? How could he acknowledge that for months and months he had been deceiving the whole parish? It was such a little thing at first, and the motive was so admirable; and yet what a fearful web it had woven around him! It had embroiled him with at least one of his parishioners; it threatened the safety of his establishment; it had ruined his life.

Regarding the cure of souls as an inefficient remedy for the social leprosy of poverty, the Doctor was a tutor first, and a clergyman afterwards, though he never lost sight of the possibility of a bishopric when useful interest was in the foreground. The Rector imparted to the tutor a good standing in society, a graceful dignity and an irreproachable character, while the mere tenure of office enabled

him to discharge his clerical functions, all
those that required any trouble being performed by Leonard Sterne who acted as the
Doctor's scapegoat generally, this no doubt
being considered in his salary.

At the same time, while the parishioners
were of secondary importance, the Doctor
was not indifferent to their opinion. He was
not content with being a potentate; he wished
to be a popular one. So far he had succeeded;
but what would be the result if Mr. Pike were
to discover the deception about Arnold and
spread it abroad? If there was any radical
change in the Doctor's nature, it was very
slight. He dreaded the scorn of the simple
villagers, the steel-vice of Mr. Valentine
Gaunt, and the possible loss of his pupils
when their parents came to hear of what had
happened; but there his repentance stopped.
It takes a great deal to grind " the old
Adam " out of a man, if indeed it ever can
be done completely.

The Doctor was very miserable—nearly
heart-broken, in fact. It seemed a hard

thing that he could not get rid of the consequences of an act which, at any rate, he
had performed with the best intentions.
Though sorry for it now, he was nevertheless
obliged to go on in the same way merely to
hide that one act; plumping down one thing
on the top of another until the whole resembled a nest of Indian boxes, almost
interminable in number, those outside very
large in size, and all for the purpose of
containing the tiniest box imaginable. Was
not there some way of throwing off this
galling yoke? The Doctor groaned as he
thought of it.

"Father!" said a gentle voice, and a soft
arm stole round his neck.

He started and looked up to behold Nellie
gazing down upon him, her blue eyes brimful
of yearning love and pity. Such a dainty
winsome maiden she looked, standing there,
nestling to his side; but oh, so pale and
sorrowful. She laid her lips upon his forehead and kissed him tenderly.

"Father, won't you tell me what troubles

you," she pleaded, "and let me help you? If
I can't help you, mayn't I suffer with you?"

"Why, darling," said the Doctor, fondly
stroking her beautiful dark hair, "what
makes you think there is anything the
matter?"

"Because I can see."

"You little rogue," he said, with his
peculiar gasping laugh. "You see far too
much at times. Those pretty eyes of yours
are apt to make very big things of very
little."

He could so easily assume this light tone
that Nellie ought not to have been surprised,
yet she looked sadly disappointed. Why
would he persist in hiding his secrets from
her? And then it occurred to her that she
was hiding a secret from him. If she were
to take him into her confidence, might it not
induce him to do the same, when perhaps
everything would be delightfully explained?
Nellie raised her head for a moment to peer
wistfully into his keen grey eyes. Then her
cheeks turned crimson, and she laid her face

against her father's, lest he should notice her confusion.

"Are you worrying about me?" she asked. "Some time ago I found that my name is not in the family Bible up there."

"Not in the family Bible!" he exclaimed in a great fluster. It was hard, terribly hard that this thing should be forced upon him when he was so anxious to turn over a new leaf. "Dear me—dear me!" said he, rubbing his forehead with his handkerchief. "What a strange omission. You have not been puzzling your dear little head over that, darling, surely?"

And now a shadow darkened the doorway, the door being open, and with stealthy tread Mr. Valentine Gaunt hovered into the room. Neither of the two by the writing-table was aware of his entrance. For a few moments he stood watching them with a sinister smile. Nellie's face was pressed lovingly against the Doctor's, and her arm was around his neck. Surely not a sight to smile at otherwise than with kindly sympathy.

" Good evening," said Mr. Valentine Gaunt.

The grouping altered instantaneously. The Doctor threw himself back in his chair with a look of alarm, while Nellie instinctively confronted the intruder as if she would protect her father from him.

CHAPTER XII.

FORCED TO MARRY.

ABOUT the time that Mr. Pike was interviewing the Doctor in Puddleton, Arnold was being received by Hebe in the drawing-room of a small house in Bayswater. Such a pretty little thing she looked, standing by the side of the great tall fellow whose arm was around her waist, her head of golden hair resting upon his breast, a smile on the bright young face, the tiny mouth slightly open, and a half-timid, half-mischievous expression in the brown eyes that watched him so anxiously. For a while they stood thus; and then she led him to a seat by the window, which looked out upon a leafy square.

It was a strange tale that she had to tell

him : a tale that stirred his blood as it had never been stirred before. And yet for her sake he was obliged to listen and answer her eager questions, just as if he knew all about it : an easier task for him with his impenetrable gravity than it would have been for many another.

Hebe, it appeared, had recently been receiving from him a number of alarming messages, imploring her to come to him at once, and even hinting that, in case she failed to comply, he contemplated putting an end to his existence with a razor. The poor girl was naturally terrified. She wrote the most pitiful letters, begging of him not to urge her to do what would certainly pain her parents, and entreating him to have patience ; but the only result in each case was another message, even more urgent than the last. She began to think his brain was affected ; many little things confirming this view were pointed out to her ; and after a desperate struggle she yielded. Indeed, she had by this time come to believe that it was her duty

to do so, in order to prevent him from laying
violent hands upon himself; she was further
influenced by the knowledge that her parents
had no objection to the marriage in itself,
while she felt confident they would forgive
her when matters were explained. Mr.
Valentine Gaunt had also assured her that
he could easily make it all right with the
Doctor, and that it would give him an excellent opportunity for reconciling father and
son. In short, Hebe had been brought to
regard her flight as an act which, though it
might cause a very brief inconvenience to
her parents, would end in a sort of general
jubilee. But, she asked Arnold, what made
him take to sending oral messages, instead
of letters?

Arnold felt that the only course open to
him was to play Mr. Valentine Gaunt's game.
He must marry Hebe just as if he actually
had sent for her. He could not put the girl
he loved to shame by telling her of the heartless fraud that had been practised upon her.
This he determined she should never know,

if he could prevent it. He must appropriate acts that he had never committed, and words that he had never uttered; he must find out by careful examination all that he was supposed to have said or done; and he must answer her awkward questions as best he could. Not that he meant to forego a reckoning with Mr. Valentine Gaunt; only it was to be managed privately, the time and manner being left to future consideration.

But then there was the question of money. He really was in a most horrible predicament. The proceeds of M. Dubarri's watch would last but a short time; his own watch might enable them to keep the wolf from the door a little longer; the rest of their belongings would scarcely fetch a ten-pound note; and after that? And yet he was thinking of marrying—could not help marrying indeed! Surely Hebe could not know his circumstances. She must have been deceived in this respect also; and if so, when she learnt how affairs really stood, she would at once suspect the whole truth, and all his en-

deavours to keep it from her would have
been in vain.

"Hebe," drawled Arnold, raising those
solemn grey eyes of his to her sunny face,
"I am not exactly a wealthy man at present."

"Oh! we shall only want a tiny, tiny
house, something like this. But we must
have a square in front, Arnold." Hebe's
notions of the value of money were somewhat
primitive. The rent of "this house" was
a hundred a year.

"In fact," he went on, reflecting her smile,
"I have nothing to do just now."

"Oh, how sweet!" cried Hebe, clasping
her little hands, and looking at him with shy
pride. "Oh, how delicious! Then I shall
have you all to myself."

"I didn't say anything about it in my
letters or messages——"

"No; but I'm so glad."

It was now evident that Mr. Valentine
Gaunt had played his cards with consummate
skill. He had said just enough for his purpose, but no more. He had calculated that

Arnold—to whom his object was a most in-comprehensible mystery—would be compelled to take up his words and deeds and marry Hebe, in spite of himself; so he had said nothing likely to lead to explanation and consequently hinder the marriage. Every-thing was turning out as he had anticipated : so carefully had his plans been laid.

"What a sweet little house that is over there!" exclaimed Hebe, enthusiastically, pointing across the square. As Arnold made no response, she added, coaxingly : "And I do declare it is to be let. Oh, Arnold, shall we take it? Look at the ivy and the low windows and the tiny conservatory, and all ; and I should so like to live near Minnie."

He had scarcely the heart to undeceive her ; but it had to be done. What would she say when he told her of the dingy house in the Harrow Road, of the duns that came round the door, of the privations within, of the visits to the pawn-shop, of a future even more terrible? How could he take her to such a scene? and yet how could he help it?

" I and a friend, M. Dubarri," he said, " have taken a furnished house by the month. He thinks it cheaper than living in lodgings : and you know, Hebe, money is a great consideration with us."

" And I am to live with you there ? " she asked, laying her hand in his.

" Yes, but perhaps you won't like it. It is a very miserable house, not at all like this ; and we—well, we don't exactly live in it. We starve in it. You see, Hebe, dear," added he, gravely looking at her bewildered face, " we are dreadfully poor, poorer than you have any idea of. We have rather got out of the way of regular meals ; we just picnic, as it were."

" Oh ; but that will be delightful," cried Hebe, who, like many others, could seldom tell whether Arnold was joking or speaking in earnest. " I detest stuck-up dinners, and I love picnics ; and then, Arnold," with a sly glance at him, " I shall have you."

" So you will ; but I should be more useful if you could eat me."

It flashed upon her that his words meant more than she had supposed. "But," she said, "I have plenty of money. See!" holding out to him an open purse, "here is all I had in the savings bank. I drew it out before I left, and you must take it; yes, please, please, to oblige me, you must."

Very gently but very firmly he put it into her pocket again. She looked disappointed at first, but soon brightened up and began to prattle about the speedy reconciliation with the Doctor, of whom she stood rather in awe. Even if he did not send them all they required, she said, her parents would, and she meant to write to them that very night in order to ease their minds and ask their forgiveness. To this Arnold offered no other objection than that she was on no account to give her address until after their marriage.

Their conversation was interrupted by the entrance of Mrs. Price, whom Hebe had spoken of as Minnie. She was a tall, handsome young widow, a born flirt, if ever there was one. She received Arnold very graciously, yet not without an amused smile. Indeed, it soon became evident that she regarded the whole affair as a capital joke ; which, however, was not the view taken by an elderly maiden aunt who lived with her.

The aunt was unmistakably attracted into the room by curiosity. While dreading contamination, she wanted to see whether the young couple who were going to make this scandalous runaway match looked and behaved like ordinary people. Keeping her eyes and ears open, she buttoned up her lips and sat rigidly erect in her chair, with her hands folded on her breast, and a look of reprobation on her prim old face.

It was about ten o'clock when Arnold left the house. The first thing that he did, after getting clear of the square, was to produce from his pocket fourpence in coppers, and to stare at them in perplexity. They represented the whole of his capital. Though he was not altogether blind to the tragic side of the picture, something very like a smile flitted across his face, as he gazed at the coins in his hand. What would M. Dubarri say, when he heard that this poverty-stricken young man, whose past had been a sealed book, was about to be married? He would go dancing mad, surely.

He found M. Dubarri sitting in the arm-chair, the black cat purring at his feet. His *pince-nez* were upon his little snub nose, for he was reading a book which he held up towards the lamp, burning dimly upon the table at his side.

Arnold thought he had never seen the room look so shabbily and scantily fur-nished before. What a melancholy contrast it formed to the bright drawing-room he had just quitted! And then the noise in the street, so different from that peaceful square. Yet these were the surroundings that he was contemplating for Hebe. He noticed that there was an ugly gap in the centre of the mantelpiece, where the American clock had lately stood. It had been removed to a chair in the corner of the room, in order, as

M. Dubarri afterwards explained, that they
might learn to do without it.

"Well, my friend?" said M. Dubarri,
eagerly laying down his book. He had not
yet succeeded in getting rid of his idea of
a possible fortune in connection with Hebe's
letter.

"I'm going to be married," announced
Arnold from the couch.

How M. Dubarri's *pince-nez* contrived to
unhook themselves from his nose, and tumble
down would be hard to explain; but the fact
that they did so will show that his features
went through some very wonderful contor-
tions. The rapidity with which his eyes
opened and closed was really astonishing.
He was still blinking when he said, like one
in a dream :

" Vous plaisantez, n'est ce pas ? "

" Not at all. I'm going to be married at
once."

" Ah-ha ! she is rich," cried M. Dubarri,
to whom no other supposition was possible.
" Sapristi ! she is rich. I congratulate you,

my friend." He sprang to his feet, and made
a wild dash at Arnold's hand. "Oh, you
dog, you are sly ! "

The tears were rolling down the old fellow's
cheeks, he was so overcome with delight.

But suddenly he turned and made a grand
bow towards the door, which had been opened
by the old shrivelled housekeeper to disclose
a suspicious-looking man, standing, hat in
hand, in the hall, and hesitating to advance.
He took courage, however, and said—

" I don't like to intrude at this hour, but it
appears to be the only time when you are at
home, and my little bill—— "

"Oh, that will be right, my dear sir,"
interrupted M. Dubarri with a lofty wave of
the hand. "Your little bill—bah ! it shall
be paid at once. We have come into our
fortune at last."

" I beg pardon, I'm sure," stammered the
man.

" Pray don't mention it, Mr. Smith. I'll
wish you a very good evening." And he
bowed out the astonished Mr. Smith, who

seemed relieved that, under the circumstances, his intrusion had been taken so quietly.

But M. Dubarri had scarcely returned to the room, when there came another knock at the door, and another suspicious-looking stranger was shown in. Although a shade of annoyance passed across M. Dubarri's face, he received the second visitor as politely as the first. In fact, the same scene was enacted over again. If this man came in rather more like a lion than the other, he certainly went out quite as much like a lamb.

"They have noses, these money-hunting fellows," said M. Dubarri; "they smell the fortune already, I think."

"I doubt it," said Arnold moodily. "More likely, they see the light in the window."

"Ah!" And he rushed to the window and closed the shutters, after which there were no more late visitors. Being far too excited to sit down, he took his stand upon the hearthrug. "Now we shall talk," he said. "So you have got a rich wife, my friend?"

" No, indeed ; that's where you have made a great mistake. The young lady is anything but rich. I might almost call her penniless."

" What! You are joking, surely. Penniless ? "

" Yes."

" Then," said M. Dubarri, almost angrily, " you are mad, I think. You must be mad. Excuse me, my friend, but you see I am frank. Who is she ? Where did she come from ? It is strange."

Arnold replied that she had stepped out of his past life. His other particulars were equally vague. He made no allusion to Mr. Valentine Gaunt's share in the matter, but took all the responsibility upon his own shoulders. As regards the future, he had no plans beyond the hope of getting employment; if that failed him—well, he kept his eyes steadily averted from this contingency.

" How will you live without money or credit ? " asked M. Dubarri, still speaking very crustily.

" We have managed badly," replied Arnold. " We ought to have taken the biggest house we could get, and then we should have lived on the fat of the land. Now, I suppose, nobody will trust us. Oh! I dare say we shall get along somehow."

" But your wife, what will she say to this miserable place? Can she eat suppers like that?" He pointed to a tray which the housekeeper had just set upon the table. It contained two herrings, a loaf of bread, and a decanter of water. " And there is worse behind. Can she live without suppers, perhaps without food?"

" It is very dreadful," admitted Arnold, " but I solemnly assure you it can't be helped. Only necessity would make me do such a thing, and we're sure to see our way out of it before long. So let us drink and be merry! But, by the way, do you object to my bringing a wife here?"

" Not at all, my dear fellow, not at all!" replied M. Dubarri, warmly shaking Arnold's hand again. " She is welcome to the little I

have. I shall do my best to make her comfortable. When will you show her to me?
I am a judge of women, you know; but I
am sure you have chosen well. Come,"
added the old fellow, smiling, " cheer up, you
great sly fellow, you! If you have no
engagement and I no pupils—that is nothing
to look gloomy at; we shall make our fortune
yet, I do assure you."

_M. Dubarri certainly kept his word. When
Hebe was introduced to him on the following
day, she was perfectly charmed with the
courteous old fellow who treated her as if she
were a duchess. There was a strange mixture
of humility and pride in his manner as he
showed her over the house, pointing out such
little things as he thought would please her,
and carefully slurring over those that would
not; and when she had seen everything, he
installed her in his armchair, and insisted
upon sending for a bottle of claret, of which
he informed her he was an excellent judge.
Once or twice, in the course of a speech in
which he proposed "long life and happiness"

to the young couple, his hand strayed to his coat as if to satisfy himself that it was buttoned; but if he thought of his absent watch and chain, this did not interfere with his good spirits.

Hebe, it must be confessed, did experience a slight chill at the first sight of her new home, but under M. Dubarri's influence and in her lover's company she very soon got over it. The novelty of the thing, also, was a great attraction. She was to be the mistress of this house. There was sweetness in that; and if the rooms might be tidier and prettier, there would be all the more scope for her when she assumed the management. In brief, she was thoroughly delighted with everything and everybody. As for M. Dubarri, there could not possibly have been a dearer old man. When she expressed this opinion to Arnold, they were walking down the Harrow Road; and happening to look back, as ladies sometimes do, she beheld M. Dubarri standing on the doorstep distributing sweetmeats to three or four little children.

After this she would have resolutely declined to hear a word against him.

The next few days glided by without any particular incident. It was arranged that the marriage should take place at the earliest possible date, and everything in the way of ceremony was to be avoided. Hebe most reluctantly promised not to spend any money on dress, and Arnold's chief preparation for matrimony was the pawning of his watch to get the wherewithal to pay the necessary fees.

END OF VOL. II.

LONDON: PRINTED BY WILLIAM CLOWES AND SONS, LIMITED, STAMFORD STREET AND CHARING CROSS.

www.ingramcontent.com/pod-product-compliance
Lightning Source LLC
Chambersburg PA
CBHW030132060726
47499CB00015B/1588